A PRIVATE MOMENT

Cat had no prior occasion in her life to see a man sleep. But she knew that if she had, it would have seemed considerably different from watching Lord Weyland now.

A warmth curled up inside her and hummed softly, like a kitten's purr. Lord Weyland was such a very . . . *lovely* man. There was something about his strong English features that drew her.

She wanted, God help her, to trace the shape of his lips with her fingertips.

Father, forgive me. She drew a slow breath, straightened her soulders, and walked up to the sleeping gentleman.

The Best Laid Plans

Laurie Bishop

A SIGNET BOOK

SIGNET
Published by New American Library, a division of
Penguin Group (USA) Inc., 375 Hudson Street,
New York, New York 10014, U.S.A.
Penguin Books Ltd, 80 Strand,
London WC2R 0RL, England
Penguin Books Australia Ltd, 250 Camberwell Road,
Camberwell, Victoria 3124, Australia
Penguin Books Canada Ltd, 10 Alcorn Avenue,
Toronto, Ontario, Canada M4V 3B2
Penguin Books (N.Z.) Ltd, Cnr Rosedale and Airborne Roads,
Albany, Auckland 1310, New Zealand

Penguin Books Ltd, Registered Offices:
80 Strand, London WC2R 0RL, England

First published by Signet, an imprint of New American Library,
a division of Penguin Group (USA) Inc.

First Printing, November 2003
10 9 8 7 6 5 4 3 2 1

In memory of my parents,
Joyce Barr Lance and Charles Kenneth Lance.
Their lives were full and well lived,
and I will always miss them.

Chapter One

"*S*top! Stop the carriage this instant!" Miss Catherine Prescott D'Eauville lurched up from her seat, grabbed the handhold, and stood as upright as she could in the bouncing vehicle—which wasn't a great deal, given Miss Catherine's imposing height. She was, however, as strong and as graceful as her nickname, and kept her feet.

"Cat, you'll fall and do yourself an injury."

"Pshaw," Cat said to her placid companion, her American cousin Rebecca Prescott. Miss Prescott was close to Cat in age, but short and delicately plump, rather like a nesting hen. "I am in perfect command of myself, Becky." Cat reached up as she spoke and knocked firmly on the roof. "I *must* see this countryside. Lovely! Does that little man hear me? Do you think he understands American knocks, or is it done differently in England?"

"I am sure we are to find out. I do believe we are slowing."

Miss Catherine stuck her elegant head out of the door as soon as it opened, hat plumes aflutter. "Yes—thank you, sir! I shall get down right here. I wish to walk about."

"Yes, mum."

In a matter of moments, Cat was down on the road, standing tall in her stylish bronze traveling gown with the black frog closures and the majestic hat—both purchased in Philadelphia expressly for her journey to her father's homeland. The hat was of velvety brown beaver with enthusiastic black and bronze plumes, and she quite liked it—when she was not riding in a confining carriage. She reached up and established that the beautiful plumes were undamaged, all the while gazing at the lovely vista that had caught her eye.

Without turning her head, she knew her cousin Becky had followed her.

"Marvelous," Cat breathed. "Lovely—almost as lovely as Virginia. Not that I have a great love of Virginia, mind you, but it is a pretty place, and cousin Martha does live there. Now, Becky, look there! Beyond those pretty rolling fields, and those trees along that very picturesque stone wall. Poplars. I believe they look like our poplars. But over there—on the rise, almost hidden by greenery—a castle. Or is it? It looks rather like one. And I don't think it is all fallen down."

"An advantage, I am sure," Becky murmured.

"What shire is this? This is still Hertfordshire, is it not? I *must* live in this county. I must marry a lord with property here. Becky, consult The List."

Cat whirled on her cousin, who, standing by the carriage in her no-nonsense gray traveling suit and her serviceable straw bonnet, was calmly opening a small leather-bound notebook. Frowning in concentration through her little gold spectacles, Becky studied it.

"These are not arranged by county, Cat."

"Oh, bother! Keep looking."

Cat turned back to the landscape, a sublime smile spreading over her face. She felt honeyed happiness in her bones. This was it, and her intuition had never guided her wrongly. Lifting her skirts, she began down the incline to the field, intent on exploring all she could of this new heaven.

"Sheep," she noted out loud, but to herself. Cat had extensive conversations with herself, and never found the company wearisome. "Very nice green grass. Very healthy grazing. And is that a stream, I wonder? I dearly love a nice trout dinner!"

She came to the bottom of the incline and began upward into the field proper, having less difficulty than she might have because of her thick-soled boots. Fashion was all very well, and she quite adored it when in the mood; but one never sacrificed practicality for it. When traveling, one wore sturdy boots.

She stopped and lifted her face, catching a scent. She stood that way a time, sorting it out. It was sweet and yet pungent, and she could not quite catch hold of it. It was a field flower, of that she was quite sure, possibly the bluish ones she saw in the distance.

"Cat!"

She heard Becky's summons and turned. Another carriage had stopped a little way behind theirs—a smaller one, a gig of some sort pulled by a single horse. A tall gentleman was making his way down the incline and coming toward her. Becky, pink-faced and clutching her skirts, was now rather desperately following him.

Cat studied the gentleman a moment, then smiled grandly and waved from her vantage point some ten yards into the field. The man, observing her wave, waved back.

Catching up her skirt once more, she walked toward him. "Hello, sir! I hope I have not committed some offense. I have no sort of weapon, as you can see."

"Please pardon me," he said. "I thought that perhaps you had difficulties."

"Why, none whatsoever! I am merely admiring this beautiful property. Do you live here?"

They met a short way from the road. Cat came to a stop before him and regarded him with cheerful amusement. He was typically English, all properly got up in a conservative dark coat, trousers and boots for traveling, a striped kerchief knotted about his throat and a top hat upon his head. He was well shaped, though, and that his refined clothes did not hide; he had shoulders as broad as a laborer's in her father's shipyard and thighs fully as sturdy. But he also held himself with perfect presence and grace, and as an added attraction, he was as tall as she was. Perhaps, he was taller. Yes, she was certain of it.

"Actually, yes. I live quite near here," he said.

He had a pleasant, well-modulated voice, she thought. Not precisely low, but in that very masculine range that made it notable—a comfortably soothing, velvety voice for a woman to hear, making one feel as though she had been given a warm cloak to wear on a cold day. He had an appealing face as well: a quiet, intelligent-looking face, a self-confident face.

"How pleasant for you. I suppose you know the owner, then?"

He raised his tawny brows slightly. At that moment he reminded her very much of her dashing cousin Tom, with his droll expression and the laugh but partially hidden in his gray eyes. "I know him intimately. He happens to be I."

"Oh." Cat eyed him with new interest. "And who might you be?"

"I am Lord Weyland."

Cat glanced over his shoulder at Becky, who waited patiently behind Lord Weyland, her breast moving visibly with her recent exertion.

"Becky, consult The List!"

Cat then looked back at Lord Weyland, who now regarded her with a mild but rather peculiar expression. She disregarded it.

"Oh, and you own all of this? How lovely! Your family must be very happy to be so *very* nicely settled."

"I myself am quite satisfied," he said. "My parents have passed on, and my sister is married and elsewhere. The park is rather extensive, and I quite like it."

Ah! Matters were fortuitous, indeed. "You are not married?"

"I am not."

"Engaged?"

"Not at present."

"Might you be an earl?"

His expression did not waiver. "I fear I am but a baron."

This was a disappointment. "Well, it must be a very old title, then."

"Well, no. My grandfather was an admiral in the navy. It was bestowed upon him. I am the third baron."

"Oh! Well, then, I'm certain the property has been in your family for years."

"I am afraid it has not. It was a purchase made by my father when Lord Durstan, the former owner, was on the rocks."

"Oh! Well, then . . . umm. . . ."

"Would you care to know my fortune?" he asked.

"Oh, no! Heavens, no. Why, I have plenty of money. That is not important at all."

Lord Weyland blinked. "I see."

In spite of the curious light in his eyes, he had such a controlled, calm, such an *English* look on his face that Cat grinned.

"Do you, then? Well, I am Catherine Prescott D'Eauville, and I have come from Boston to find myself a proper lord to marry. Or perhaps I should put it differently? I suppose that sounds a trifle brazen to English ears." She extended her hand with an enthusiastic flourish.

She meant to give him a suitable American handshake, but Lord Weyland reached out and took her gloved hand in his. Then he bowed over it—and grazed her knuckles lightly with his lips.

He raised his head and met her gaze. "A trifle brazen, perhaps," he murmured. "Here we say 'I am seeking an eligible *parti*.' "

Cat barely noticed the twinkle in his eyes. She was too much taken up with the fascinating sensation of having had her hand kissed, just *so*, by an agreeable gentleman. In the space of an instant, she realized what she had missed among the young men of Boston, who had wonderful manners, to be sure—but there was a certain difference.

Yes, my girl, there surely is.

"Well!" she said at last. "I am staying at present with my English cousin and his wife, I believe a very short way from here—I am a bit turned around, I fear. They are situated in Shallcross. My American cousin, Miss Prescott, and I arrived these several days past, were rested by breakfast the next morning, and are having the grandest time exploring! Now Charl—um, my cousin, our host—shall set about inviting the neighborhood to visit, I daresay. I do believe all have been apprised of my arrival, so some little party or other should not take long to arrange. In any event, you should come by, Lord Weyland, and we need not even confess we have met and not been properly introduced." She smiled again.

Lord Weyland's lips, to this moment disciplined into a firm line, curved upward ever so slightly. "We need not—that is true."

"Then you shall come."

"I presume your cousin is Lord Ralston."

"Oh—yes. Did I not say so?"

"You did not," Lord Weyland said, "but I understand Lord Ralston to be entertaining an American cousin at home."

She smiled. "Yes, you are quite right."

"Then I shall happen by." He stepped back. "Perhaps I should follow your carriage as far as the turning."

"Absolutely not. Miss Prescott and I are quite the independent women! Besides, my driver knows the way." She stepped past Lord Weyland to join her patient cousin, who stood waiting like a handmaiden to royalty. "Good day, Lord Weyland!"

"Good day."

They reached the road, and Cat climbed into the carriage beside Becky. All in all Cat was satisfied with her adventure so far, but sorely regretful of one thing.

"There is no Lord Weyland on The List," Becky murmured. The most agreeable Lord Weyland did not fit her criteria.

The carriage began to roll, and Cat gazed out the window at the lovely field they left behind. She could no longer see the tall gentleman with the smile in his eyes.

"Good heavens, cousin, you never allowed a man to accost you at the side of the road!"

Cat gazed across her cousin Charles's elegant dinner table at the gentleman himself, a sturdy, sandy-haired fellow some years her senior who bore, she felt, little resemblance to her father. It was a pity, for Father was a handsome man who still turned feminine heads at the age of eight and forty. Still, Charles did not favor his uncle, and so that was that.

"Do not fuss, dearest," said Lady Ralston. "She has only just arrived in our home."

"But this is important." Lord Ralston stabbed a piece of cold ham on his plate. "Our duty is to see her properly wed to a man of station if not of means. It is the charge we accepted. It is going to be a difficult thing if Miss D'Eauville acts in such a way as to diminish herself in the eyes of society."

"Miss Prescott was with her," said his wife.

For her part, Becky sat quietly pursuing her plate, apparently paying little attention to the discussion.

"Dear, dear," Cat said. "I have caused such a flutter already. Dear Charles, do not fret. I am not a goose. I am two and twenty and attended Madame Victorine's Finishing School in Boston, and I assure you I am up to snuff."

"If that were true, you would address me as *Lord Ralston*, as is proper!"

"Oh, pshaw, how can I not call you Charles? You were naught but Charles that whole year you stayed with us!"

"*Lord* Charles," Charles huffed. "And you refused to call me anything but Charles."

"Poor dear Charles," said Cat. "I have been so trying to you so soon! But as to the gentleman I encountered, I appraised him immediately, quite thoroughly, and knew I was perfectly safe. As to what society thinks— cousin, I present myself as exactly what I am. I am an American heiress willing to marry impoverished English nobility. There are any number of them, and they shall not be concerned over my meetings at sides of roads."

"Good Lord—that fellow could be anybody!" snapped Charles. "I'll wager you did not get his name!"

"Your language, dearest," said Lady Ralston.

"What matter is it if I did not get his name? I supposed I would not see him again, of course." Cat smiled. It would be such a good joke if Lord Weyland did pay a call; although she supposed they would keep their first meeting a secret between them.

She hoped he *would* come.

"And pray remember to address me as Lord Ralston," Charles sputtered. "I am driven to question that finishing school you attended."

"Let her eat, dear," said Lady Ralston.

"My love, the matter of Miss D'Eauville's meeting gentlemen *is* an issue of moment. We do not want her frightening them off!"

"No, you are thinking in the wrong way, Charles," Cat said. "I shall rather make certain demands of *them*. They must be of sufficient status, but I must control my money, go where I please and do as I please. And"— Cat broke her speech and frowned into space—"he must be pleasing to me." Satisfied, she forked into a bit of jellied lamb.

"The poor devil will wonder what he has got himself into," muttered Charles. He reached for his goblet.

"Charles, do you remember the jackass you rode at cousin Martha's plantation?" Cat said benignly. "The one I promised you would give you a surprise?"

Lady Ralston burst out in a laugh.

"I do not recall being amused!" Charles said. "*Lord Ralston*, If you please!"

Susan, Lady Ralston took up her napkin and pressed it to her lips. More giggles emerged. She was a thin, pale woman with gray threading too early through her blond hair, but Cat thought her laughing eyes brought out her natural beauty. Cat smiled at her. She quite liked Charles's wife. There was nothing prim or pricklish about her.

"*I* had never ridden that jackass," Cat went on. "I knew better. And my perception, I assure you, extends to men."

"Preposterous," sputtered Charles. "Comparing finding a gentleman to marry with finding a jackass to ride!"

Lady Ralston was near helpless with giggles now. Becky, ever reserved, sat quietly eating her dinner, as if the outrageous dinner conversation bothered her not at all.

"Well," Charles said, attacking his plate once again, "I shall follow your father's wishes and gather up all of the eligible men. And they may bray and kick as they like, and you may pick the best of the lot. We shall saddle you a Lord Jackass, cousin, and then we all shall be happy again."

Cat threw back her head and laughed. She was enjoying herself. She dearly loved Charles; and even after a separation of some seven years, she did so love to tease him. He did not, for all his bluster, have an unkind bone in his body . . . and she also knew that her father's trust in him was not misplaced.

Charles would undoubtedly find her a future husband.

Subject to her approval, of course. Miss Catherine Prescott D'Eauville had great plans, oh, yes . . . and they required an *obedient* husband. Father would be peaceful at last, and she would be established in the world with her prodigious great lord and seek her grand adventure.

What more could a maiden wish for?

Chapter Two

"*Tell* me, Jack, what sort of a young woman is she, this American Miss D'Eauville?" Miss Beatrice Southrop continued working on her intricate lacework, not looking up.

John Weyland, Lord Weyland, watched the afternoon sun make glints of gold in Aunt Bea's flaxen hair. He sat companionably near her in his favorite armchair in the pleasant west parlor, whose windows overlooked the garden; a warm breeze brushed in through the open casements, and he felt very content this evening. It had been an exceptionally interesting day.

"There is an engaging liveliness about her. She is a curious mixture of refinement and the unanticipated, and I think she is rather used to managing herself. Certainly, she is full of self-assurance."

Aunt Bea tsk-tsked. "She sounds quite wild. She does not seem the kind of wife a man would want to present to the polite world."

Jack felt himself smile. "Ah, but the polite world does not live with one and sleep in one's bed. I should not call her wild. I found her to be quite interesting."

"And so I detect." Aunt Bea looked up and favored him with a stare that said much. "What does she look like?"

"Hmm." Jack visualized her, and again he felt the smile. His Interesting American was no Pocket Venus.

"She is tall, exquisitely formed, with rich brown hair and the most beautiful brown eyes. She is by far the healthiest specimen of womanhood I have viewed in quite some time."

"She resembles her father," said Aunt Bea. "That is it, then. You are blinded by appearances. Jack, my boy, at eight and twenty you should know much better." Aunt Bea turned her attention back to her lacework, obscuring her face from Jack's view. "One in your position weds with care. You have much to your advantage, and it can gain you a very eligible wife."

Poor Aunt Bea. She *would* have him wed—to a duke's daughter if she had the deciding of it.

"As to that, she was very clear that she is seeking a husband with better pedigree than mine, so you need not worry on that head."

"Ah, I see how it is! I should have deduced as much. The apple does not fall far from the tree."

"You have not seen Lionel D'Eauville in a quarter of a century, and you were a child then. You cannot have known him so well as all that. And certainly, you can not know his daughter."

Aunt Bea made a dismissive sound. "Never mind. As if you are in the least way interested in a wife. Each time a good possibility comes your way, you make haste to escape it. You had much rather be off meddling with your animals or tinkering with one of your odd ideas. I shall be in the Hereafter before I see any grandnieces and grandnephews."

"Aunt Bea, my dear," he said mildly, "I know how much my meddling and tinkering annoys you. But, in truth, I would much rather share a beautiful evening in your company than in that of any young flower I have met."

"Jack, you are a foolish boy, and I am much too old and wise for that nonsense. You may tell it to your horse."

Jack chuckled. "I do love you, Aunt Bea. And I shall try harder to find a wife. For you, I shall."

"The proof is in the pudding," she said.

The proof was in the pudding, indeed, Jack thought, smiling to himself as he drove his gig up before the impressive Ralston estate. It was true that he was not anxious to wed; his life was fully absorbing as it was, and he hated any unnecessary distraction from his various studies and projects. That was not to say, however, that he could not enjoy an excursion such as this one—an invitation to Ralston Hall for what promised to be a most interesting house party, welcoming the American cousin Miss Catherine D'Eauville to England. Jack was an observer, and as an observer he loved to go anywhere that promised to provide interesting spectacles and curiosities. He was sincerely thankful to his friend Ralston for this opportunity.

Ralston Hall had long been a local landmark, with its regal gothic facade and spacious manicured grounds—although a bit pretentious for Jack's taste, which was more compatible with his own ancient stone manor home. As if to illustrate his thoughts, two liveried grooms came for his gig before his horse had scarcely stopped. Charles was surely putting on appearances for the occasion of his cousin's introductory party, Jack thought, even if the old boy did tend to go for the formalities in a general way. Ralston enjoyed being an earl, with all the accompanying pomp and circumstance, whether he could afford it or not.

Jack got down and soon found himself let into the spacious hall by a very superior butler, a footman who took his hat and gloves, and a footman who took his coat. Jack thought humorously that if he were to begin unfastening his trousers, another footman would appear.

"If you would come with me, sir," the butler said.

"Never mind. I shall find my own way." Jack set off and the butler allowed it, as the butler, Mr. Penn, had known Jack for the past twenty-odd years—since the first time that young Jack had scaled the Ralston garden wall. Jack and Charles had been friends from that day onward.

Jack walked down the wide marble hall toward the faint sounds of voices. It was early afternoon yet, and all the guests would not have arrived. The men would be in the billiard room or, perhaps, examining the stables; and the ladies would be in the drawing room, in one parlor or the other, or in the garden. Jack decided on the drawing room.

He had made the correct guess. In the company of several other ladies was Miss Catherine D'Eauville, holding the others captive with an animated monologue. Jack stopped inside the doorway, and after taking his fill of Miss D'Eauville's lovely and enlivened face, he cast a glance around at the others.

Lady Ralston looked properly attentive; Miss Halstead seemed confused; Mrs. Barbury looked faintly disapproving; Miss Carter looked fascinated; Lady Mackley seemed to be trying to decide how she should look.

"And do you know, the bull simply stood grazing while little Billy toddled right past him. Martha was near to fainting. The farmhands stood around like statues. I thought then to pick up the bucket of oats Ben had for the mare that had just given birth and straightaway began to tempt him with it. The bull, I mean."

Jack raised his hand to hide a smile.

"Lord. What happened then?" asked Miss Carter.

"Well," Miss D'Eauville said, demonstrating with her hands, "I rattled the bucket at the fence and called Mr. Bull in the nicest tones. He looked at me, and I think he was so surprised that I was offering him something good. He at length began to come toward me. I then signaled to the workmen, and they understood exactly what to do."

Miss D'Eauville came to her feet, holding her hands out in pantomime. "I kept coaxing the bull, and one of them ran out and snatched little Billy right up and made for the fence as fast as he could. It was a close-run thing!"

Miss D'Eauville looked about at the circle of watchers, and finally her gaze came to the doorway. There it stopped, and she stood in her pretty yellow muslin afternoon gown, her hand outstretched holding an imaginary bucket of oats, regarding him.

"Good afternoon, ladies," Jack said, stepping into the room. "I have just arrived, and I wished to pay my respects."

"Lord Weyland!" exclaimed Lady Ralston, getting to her feet. "Welcome! Ralston will be very glad to see you." She stepped toward him in a flutter of lavender, her thin face alight with pleasure.

Jack smiled at her, but it was not Lady Ralston that his attention was for. In his peripheral vision, Jack saw Miss D'Eauville lower the bucket of oats.

Lady Ralston warmly took his hand. "Let me introduce our guest, Ralston's cousin from Boston, Miss Catherine D'Eauville."

There was no doubting his previous conclusion—Miss D'Eauville was a very healthy specimen of woman. He gazed at her standing there in lovely frothy yellow, at how she stood perhaps a head taller than Lady Ralston, and at how the yellow muslin floated over what appeared to be fine rounded hips and a remarkably dainty waist, and how, above this, her bosom filled her bodice to feminine perfection.

Miss D'Eauville was more woman than he had ever seen; and in his eyes, the most womanly. Certainly, she was worth his study.

She was recovered. "Lord Weyland," she said cheerfully. "How very nice to meet you." She came to him and extended her hand.

He took it, smiling into her remarkably bright brown

eyes. "A pleasure, Miss D'Eauville. I gather you have recently arrived."

"Only the sennight past," she said with perfect ease, as though in truth speaking to him for the first time. "My cousin Miss Prescott and I have entertained ourselves touring the most interesting roads. We have seen such marvelous sights." Her eyes twinkled with amusement.

"I am very glad of that," he said. He kissed her hand, and looked in time to see the faint blush covering her lightly tanned cheeks. He hadn't imagined it before, then. The lively Miss D'Eauville had a streak of maidenly shyness. A very narrow streak, to be sure, but she had one.

"Do you know Lord Ralston well?" she asked.

He released her hand. "Very. We spent our boyhoods together."

"Lord Weyland is our most frequent visitor," said Lady Ralston. "Although, more often to the stables than to the house!"

"Really?" Miss D'Eauville favored Jack with a most inquisitive expression. "Are you very interested in horses?"

"He is fascinated by them," said Lady Ralston. "And anything with four legs, or with two and feathers. But usefully so, I must admit. His advice saved Ralston's best mare a fortnight ago."

Admiration was instant on Miss D'Eauville's face, open and genuine. "You must tell me about this!" she said.

"Do not entice him with the subject of animals!" Lady Ralston said with a laugh. "Or for that matter, with any thing vegetable or mineral. He can be quite carried off by his science!"

"I promise I shall tell," Jack said. He leaned forward just slightly, with a mock-serious expression. "—at a more propitious time."

Jack liked the genuine spark of interest in Miss

D'Eauville's eyes. He also liked the golden cast to her skin, which spoke of time out-of-doors with less than the usual female caution against the sun; and he liked the way her rich mahogany hair was piled into a loose coiffure, at once carefree and enticing, and gleaming brightly wherever caught by the light. A string of pearls glowed like pebbles of ice against her golden throat; he wanted to touch them, to see if they would melt.

In all truth, he wanted to touch Miss D'Eauville and see if *she* would melt. But being a gentleman had its limitations . . . particularly a gentleman of science.

"I think," she said in her distinctly low, musical voice, "that we must speak of your interests, and very soon. Yes, I should like that very much."

"I think it is time for tea," said Lady Ralston. "Shall we have it here, or would we prefer the garden?"

Miss D'Eauville turned to her. "Oh, I should like to go out-of-doors. It is an excellent day today. I cannot be indoors too long!" She turned back to Jack at this. "Would you like to walk out, Lord Weyland? I am already quite in love with the garden. Oh, I suppose you are quite familiar with it."

"I am, and I walk in it at every opportunity." He extended his arm. "Shall we take a tour?"

He was cognizant of the speculative looks of the ladies, of which Miss D'Eauville seemed unaware. He was certain that if she were, however, she would not consider it of consequence.

"Yes, let us do. Susan, will you send our tea into the garden?" She took his arm readily, and shortly they were walking out onto the back terrace as if the oldest of friends. Jack felt no self-consciousness from her, only her true enjoyment; for himself, he admired the way she moved at his side with such strength and grace, an elegant combination in a woman.

"You seem to be happily arranged," he said as they descended the flagstone steps into the garden. "How go your marital plans?"

She glanced up at him, giving him a wry look through thick lashes, but not at all a coquettish look. She smiled in good humor. "Heaven knows as yet. Charles is summoning all the candidates in easy travel distance, and I shall have quite a time for myself, I should think."

"So should I."

"So should you . . . ?"

He smiled. "Have a time of it. This is quite the interesting event for our little neighborhood."

"Excellent. I dearly love to entertain."

"I hope you shall as dearly love your results."

"Do you mean my marriage?"

"Of course."

"Oh, that is nothing. It is simply a matter I must attend to. It will do well enough."

"My dear Miss D'Eauville." He stopped them on the garden path and turned to her, looking straight into her expressive eyes. "Do you mean your marriage is not of paramount importance to you? That it is not to be the culmination of maidenly dreams?"

She searched his face, and then, apparently learning what she wanted in some mystic way, she grinned. "Is that what all men think? Goodness, no. My dreams are much grander, I assure you. I wish to travel. I wish to climb mountains. I wish to ride upon an elephant. I wish to cross a gypsy's palm with silver. Why should I be any different than you?"

"Indeed."

He studied her smiling face and felt a curious tightening in his chest. She was a very different sort of woman, indeed. In short, he was inspired to even greater curiosity about Miss D'Eauville.

"Then, if I may ask, why marry at all? You have already crossed an ocean. You may continue your adventures without the baggage of a husband."

"Oh, but that *is* a problem. I have to be respectable, you see. And Father is quite set on it. I think he always felt he should have been Lord Ralston, even if he was the youngest brother; so now that he has made his fortune, he wants me to insure that his grandchildren are of the most exceptional title. I can see no reason not to please him."

She did not seem quite serious; her eyes danced. And yet he sensed a deep truth within them. "So the title is of no great consequence to you?"

"Not particularly. I am quite content as I am. In Boston, being Miss Catherine Prescott D'Eauville is quite burdensome enough! But Father is the dearest man in the world, and that makes all the difference."

Jack was beginning to see. Miss D'Eauville was not driven by social ambition, but by love and loyalty—and a curious indifference to the married state she sought. This did seem to fit better with her character as he perceived it. She was a fascinating subject.

He took her arm, and they continued up the pretty path. A tall hedge of yew now guarded their view of the manor; a gust of evening air brushed her jonquil skirts against his legs as they walked.

"So tell me," he asked, "do you anticipate any of your guests with special interest?"

She hesitated in answer, but only for a bare moment. The soft breeze brushed a stray strand of her upswept hair so it danced on her forehead; she seemed not to notice.

"In fact, there is a certain Lord Carlisle on The List who seems quite acceptable."

Her voice was cheerful, as offhand as before.

"Carlisle. Hm. He is perhaps six and twenty, medium height, somewhat fleshy, and quite pompous. His father lost much of the family fortune gaming, and Carlisle would be most interested in a profitable marriage. I suspect he has inherited his father's gambling traits, however."

"That is disappointing," she said. "But there is Lord Whitby."

"Thirties, quiet, managed by his widowed mother, and some say lacking in wits."

"Lord Johnston."

"A pleasant fellow. A good-looking gentleman of twenty-two or -three."

"Is that all?"

"I do not know him well."

"Well, you have no bad news of him, at least. I was beginning to think I would not have your good opinion of any of them."

"My good opinion, once granted, is well earned, Miss D'Eauville."

She raised her brows at him, an amused sparkle in her eyes. He caught the fleet scent of jasmine.

"How very superior of you, Lord Weyland. Do you come by your excellent knowledge by nature, or by endeavor?"

"Why, by a generous measure of both, Miss D'Eauville. I am a remarkably intelligent man, and I have used my mental capabilities to my own best benefit."

She laughed delightfully, and giving herself to her feeling in full measure, released his arm and turned about in a full, graceful circle while the notes of her pleasure pealed like bells. They came to a stop within a grove of apple trees. The sun was beginning its afternoon descent, lengthening shadows and spilling golden light in which the bees danced; it caught her in its happy glow.

She turned back to him as the warm breeze brought him a waft of sweet honeysuckle. "Tell me, then," she said, "how does such a superior gentleman as yourself while away his time? I think it must be with your science that I was warned against speaking of."

"By all means, do not bring it up. I may begin to speak on irrigation."

"Heavens!"

"Or husbandry."

"Shocking."

"Or, I might invite you to see my newest clever device of my making—a combination walking stick, compass, and spyglass."

"Dear me! I am in a fine predicament now, for I do wish to see that walking stick!" Miss D'Eauville laughed aloud again, enjoyment of him clear in her eyes.

"Seriously, sir, what things do interest you? Is it agriculture and clever inventions, then?"

"It is much more than that." He had not intended it, but he was drawn into giving her a more honest account of himself. "All things fascinate me. There is endless diversion. Man himself is such a source of inspiration that I could devote myself entirely to his study."

"How interesting. What aspect of man do you study?"

They began walking again, and whether Jack started off first, or if she did, he did not notice. He focused on his answer, for it somehow seemed very important, and she seemed rapt on his response.

"I study man from all perspectives. I am convinced that one's innate qualities together with what one is taught, what one does, and what one eats all decide what a man is—that is to say, his health, his mental capacity, and his character."

"I see. Well, I should think that if a man were born to be king, it would not matter what he eats."

"It should not offset that destiny, unless he should die before he assumes the throne. But the other elements should certainly affect how well he performs as a ruler."

"Very well. But if I may say so, I believe your king's condition has come from more than what he eats or what he was taught."

Miss D'Eauville was not shy about entering the delicate political arena; it did not surprise him. Clearly, however, it was up to him to steer them to a safer subject.

"Perhaps if we may leave His Royal Highness for a . . . hm . . . better example? Let us consider a horse. You are knowledgeable about animals, are you not?"

She grinned. "Yes."

"If you wished to breed an excellent mount, would you choose a sire or a dam who was bodily or mentally unsound?"

"Of course not."

"Even if his bloodlines were good to your knowledge?"

"It would not matter. If the horse is a poor specimen of beast, I should not choose it for breeding."

"Now let us take your prize foal, which for the purpose of our discussion, we will assume you have obtained. If you were to feed it poorly and treat it ill, would it become the excellent mount you desire?"

"No, it would not."

"Then I have proven my case. Man is as any other beast; all things have a hand in making him the person he is."

"And you make a study of this."

"I do not in a consuming way. It is but one idle occupation. One is entertained by developing interesting theories; but one is well served by a walking stick."

"Ah," she said. "Then you are not suggesting that I choose a husband the way I would choose a horse?" She gazed at him smiling, her expression anticipatory.

"Heavens, no. We all know man is such a very superior animal, above such paltry considerations. And how could you ever make sure of all that your gallants eat?"

She laughed again. "Or whether they were beaten by their nurse or locked in dark cellars for days on bread and water? I could ask them, but I think that would not answer!"

"Precisely. So science is best left to the scientists, my dear Miss D'Eauville."

"Oh, there I disagree. If I wish a gentleman's character to be detected, I shall insist upon being fully included. There are things in which I trust my own judgment much more than I will another's opinion."

"I fully understand. Very laudable of you, I daresay."

Yes indeed, Miss D'Eauville would have the managing of her selection of beaux as her father waited, unsuspecting, on the other side of the ocean. Or . . . perhaps her father was fully aware of his daughter's propensity to arrange matters to suit herself. He pondered on this, wondering if a daughter's loving facade, and a father's loving blindness, could perhaps render that untrue.

The path emerged from the shade of a giant juniper, and they had circled around to where they had started. Jack felt a surprising jab of disappointment as the back terrace of Ralston loomed, but the sight of Lady Ralston hurrying toward them quickly superseded it.

"There you are! Lord Weyland, you are very bad, keeping Miss D'Eauville away for so very long! Your tea is cold, but that is not what I have come searching for you to say." She stopped before them, breathless and enlivened with her excitement. She turned to Miss D'Eauville. "Lord Macclesby has arrived, and is most anxious to meet you, cousin. Perhaps you would wish to change?"

The courtiers are arriving, then. Jack wished they had only a bit more time together. There was much he wished to know about this enchanting American; much he wished to study. And, he had to admit, he did enjoy her company.

"Oh, no," she said. "I shall wear this dress. And you may tell Lord Macclesby that when I have finished my delightful tour of your garden and my conversation, I shall be pleased to meet him."

Damn, if he didn't think he quite liked Miss Catherine Prescott D'Eauville.

Chapter Three

$\mathcal{T}$he draperies of the drawing room were closed and candles lit against the coming evening; the mellow glow played off polished wood and sparkling crystal goblets and twinkled in the jewels of the ladies.

In addition to Catherine, there were present her courtiers—Lord Macclesby of course, and a Lord Swain and a Lord Rhodes; and Susan, Rebecca, and two other ladies also made part of the party. Too, Charles and Lord Weyland had of late joined them, seating themselves in the remaining chairs near the door. They were not conveniently in Cat's vision, but she was perfectly aware of their presence—particularly, of Lord Weyland's.

Macclesby was just such a lord as her father wanted for her. Cat had done her research, and he met her criteria very well. He was to inherit an earldom, and his father's estate, although sadly encumbered, was on a lovely piece of green and rolling land to the south. Additionally, the manor itself was pleasingly grand—she had been told it was in part an ancient abbey, built on in subsequent years, with both an Elizabethan and a Georgian wing. She had heard, too, that there were many grand and old furnishings that had not yet gone to settle debt. Of course, he was facing financial ruin. It seemed she could not choose better.

Still, it was most frustrating that she must hold her

attention to the very eligible Lord Macclesby. The said gentleman was tall and spare and a Dandyish dresser; his green silk cutaway coat and snug mustard yellow trousers did nothing to disguise his length of thin leg. In all, he gave her the impression of a spider—even more so at the present, for he was seated in a Queen Anne chair with his knees decidedly higher than they ought to be. Additionally, he had a very pointed nose, and was forever rubbing the side of it with his forefinger, which Cat would have minded less if he were not talking so incessantly of himself.

The fact that she had that very evening enjoyed an agreeable interlude with a handsome English gentleman in a lovely English garden had something to do with it, she was afraid; and Lord Weyland *was* handsome. She had straightaway concluded this, she decided, upon her first gaze into his intelligent gray eyes. How perverse of him to be but an insignificant baron, living on an estate acquired from some unfortunate wastrel, likely at a bargain price! And he *would* have to be agreeable and amusing and clever.

"Queen Elizabeth once stayed in our Royal Bedchamber," Lord Macclesby was saying, "and my family has not changed it at all since then. She told my ancestral host that she quite liked the room and that it should not be altered, you see. The rugs, the draperies are left the same. There is yet velum in the writing desk that she used."

"She would be quite pleased, then, if she could return," Cat said. She cast him a most innocent expression. "I hope it is not all moths."

"Oh, certainly not," he said with alacrity. "We take great care of that room. It is regularly aired and thoroughly dusted, and a fire is lit in the grate from time to time."

"Ah! Then it would not make one sneeze. I understand your Prince Regent is rather susceptible to ailments."

"My dear Miss D'Eauville, we would not place our prince in those chambers. We would show him to a modern room, especially fit for him."

"Gracious, it is fortunate you do not have *too* many royal visitors. You should soon run out of rooms altogether."

There was an intake of breath from near the door, then a cough. Cat knew just whose cough it was. Lord Weyland was being entertained, and likely surmising what Lord Macclesby had eaten for breakfast.

"Lord Swain," Cat said pleasantly to the other gentleman, "had you a room for Queen Elizabeth?"

The young man blushed and looked distressed. "I think not. That is, there must be one. Place is old as Adam. I do not know which room it is, I must say."

"Queen Elizabeth did not visit everyone," Macclesby said dryly.

"I-I have a very nice orangery," said Lord Rhodes.

Cat looked at him and smiled. "An orangery? That is interesting."

Lord Rhodes had been quiet until now. Middle-aged, of a sturdy and slightly fleshy build, and unprepossessing in nature, he might have gone unnoticed. Cat, however, found him more appealing than the pompous Macclesby and the very young Lord Swain.

"My mother is very fond of it," Lord Rhodes said.

"I have seen it," said Lady Ralston. "It is very pleasant. It is a pity, though, it is such a very far ride from here. You would like it, Miss D'Eauville."

"An orangery?" Macclesby drawled. "I believe we have one. But of course. It is very large. We have dozens of exotic potted trees that we keep there each winter. It is much remarked upon."

"B-blight gets them." Lord Swain tugged nervously at his neckcloth.

Macclesby stared at him. "What?"

"Blight." Lord Swain swallowed. "Gets the trees."

"Not *my* trees, I must say!"

"I do believe," said Cat, "that Lord Weyland is the gentleman to discuss blight with." She cast Lord Weyland a smiling glance. In the brief moment their gazes interlocked. "He is a man of science, I understand."

Lord Weyland's eyes twinkled at her, but the whole of his face remained as immovable as ever.

"Blight," Lord Weyland said, "is a very serious and tricky business. So much so, that I hesitate to speak of it before the ladies."

"I see no need to speak of it at all," drawled Macclesby. Reluctantly, Cat looked back at him. Macclesby leaned back in his chair and raised his chin in a superior manner.

"But you do disappoint Miss D'Eauville," said Weyland. "A dilemma, indeed."

Macclesby colored, Charles coughed, and the ladies tittered. Cat, for her part, stood up, possessed of a sudden need to escape. Her enjoyment of the absurd, after all, had its limits.

"I need to move about. Perhaps we may have music or a game." She turned to Susan. "Agreed?"

Lady Ralston looked confused for a second, then rose to the occasion. "Of course. I shall have the whist tables set up."

Whist! My sweet heaven. Cat smiled at Susan, then glanced around the room. Her gaze settled on Rebecca. Yes, that would do.

"My dear Becky! Do you feel quite well?"

Becky widened her eyes slightly and favored Cat with a look of tolerant inquiry.

"Oh, I am so sorry!" Cat exclaimed. "I have been so sunk in my own pleasure that I had forgot you are suffering. How is your headache now, dear?" Cat continued to hold Becky in a fixed gaze.

Becky blinked slowly. "I do believe . . . that it has quite come back. I think that perhaps I should go lie down."

"Yes, you should." Cat advanced upon Becky with

determination. "And I shall attend to you. My poor Becky, how you do put up with me."

There was an immediate stir in the room, and exclamations of regret and consolation. Becky protested that Cat must not interrupt herself; Cat countered that she would see to Becky's comfort and would not be made to do otherwise. In a moment she had the ailing Becky's arm, and the two ladies crossed to the doorway.

Lord Weyland stood with Charles as they passed; and then Lord Weyland caught her eye. To Cat's chagrin, he winked at her. Before she could respond, he nodded at Rebecca.

"With Miss D'Eauville as your nursemaid," he said gently, "we shall be certain of your *very* rapid recovery."

Cat turned regally away, and tugging at Becky's elbow, drew her out into the hall.

"Whatever can he mean by that?" Cat said as they neared the stairs.

Becky raised a brow. "I think he means that he apprehends I am perfectly well, and that you are perfectly bored."

"Of course he does," snapped Cat. "Which makes no matter at all! It only matters that no one else does, and well he knows it. I think he means to tease me."

To that, Becky answered not at all.

Cat awoke early. In the space of a moment she recognized her room, the high-ceilinged chamber of faded grandeur in which her cousin Charles had housed her; and recalling that there were some two dozen guests in the house, counting among them the three aspiring swains, Cat felt a sudden urge to be rid of them. This, of course, she could not do, but to shake the sense of confinement was an absolute necessity, particularly after the previous agonizingly dull evening. Therefore, she chose to go exploring.

Cat slipped out of the cavernous canopy bed and

whisked up her robe as the damp cool of morning penetrated her cotton gown. The rosy light through the French windows indicated the sun had risen, although the maid had not yet removed her chamber pot.

She had but cold water in her pitcher from the night before, but she enjoyed the shock of it on her skin. Next she dressed her own hair in a simple style, and only then did she summon her wondering maid to assist with donning her riding dress. In a relatively short time indeed she let herself out into the fresh air of an English morning.

Rather than send for her mount, she chose to walk to the stables. It was thus she surprised a stable boy mucking out one in a long row of stalls.

He straightened, planted his fork, and blushed. She observed him with sympathetic amusement. He had the reddest hair she had ever seen, and his complexion matched it.

"Do I frighten you?"

"No, ma'am."

"Good. I need a task from you. Can you saddle the mare I rode the other day?"

His eyes bulged, and he began to stammer.

Cousin Charles had warned her never to ride without a groom, but in this he had wasted his breath. Cat had no intention of spoiling her pleasure. The stable boy was no match for her; in moments he happily performed as he was bid, completely reassured.

She pointed her mare Daphne in the direction of the interesting rolling hills to the southwest, and as soon as the horse was limber and warm, urged her to a canter.

Sweet moist wind brushed her face, and she rose and fell to her mare's lovely rhythm. A sea chantey entered her head and played with its frolicsome lyric:

> *A drink to my fulsome Weymouth maid, round*
> *and brown as a barrel. A drink to her goodly*
> *father's grave, a drink to the church where she'll*

marry. A drink to her babes and her warm
feather bed, and a drink to the sea where I'll tarry.

Cat smiled, breathing in the earth and grass scent, her eyes full of the palette of greens of field, wood, and hedgerow and the wispy white afloat in the blue above. And more—it was cool as she liked it, although she was warming now with exertion.

Her mare topped a rise, and at the vista beyond Cat reined her in.

Ah. It was none other than her discovery of the week before—Lord Weyland's enchanting property.

Delighted, Cat scanned the landscape with a sense of proprietary pleasure. She was not surprised; she had learned Lord Weyland's direction as the bird flew, which was not so very far from cousin Charles's estate, and had taken that way this morning.

It was just *so* unfortunate that Lord Weyland did not belong to the history of the place in any enduring way. And it was doubly unfortunate that his ancestors had not been more ambitious. Goodness, his family had done nothing for centuries until his seafaring grandfather had become a baron. *Her* grandfather had been the fifth Earl of D'Eauville, no less, and *she* was a common American!

Weyland's wife would be *Lady* Weyland, of course . . .

Cat gazed across the green dale at the ancient stone hall and fought the twinge of regret. There was no object in her thoughts dwelling there, not with her important mission at stake. Dear Father's happiness and her own future satisfaction depended upon her adhering to The List like a novice to her vows. Still . . .

Still, with its round corner towers and numerous gables, Lord Weyland's home was impressive. It had four floors with many tall mullioned windows and a semicircular drive planted with sentinel trees. Upon its wide expanse of neatly trimmed park were numerous attractive outbuildings, including, she was quite certain, an orangery. That thought made her smile. Perhaps Lord Weyland had a bedroom where Queen Elizabeth had slept, as well.

Of course, the queen would have necessarily been the guest of the family of the dissolute heir who had sold the whole to a sailor-turned-baron.

Still smiling to herself, Cat urged her mare down the hill, full of the urge to explore Lord Weyland's domain. Her father must know this property, she thought; she would write him about it. It was a certainty he had ridden over this very land as a child. Had he known Lord Weyland's family?

As she drew closer, she noted that the manor and grounds had a decided air of prosperity, which piqued her curiosity. It was in the neatness of the place, the good repair of the buildings, the carefully pruned shrubbery. It appeared that Lord Weyland was a prudent caretaker, and he was certainly to be admired for that—although she did not know if the attention to appearances extended to the inside of the place. She found herself wishing very much, then, that she could see the interior of Lord Weyland's domain.

The wish, no sooner conceived, was determined upon. But how to do so was indeed a problem. She could scarce present herself at the door alone, even if Lord Weyland were not at home—which he was not, as he had spent the night at Charles's estate.

Cat urged her mare forward at a leisurely pace, following the crest of the low ridge that skirted the front of Weyland Hall. She fell deep into contemplation, her quick mind turning bits and pieces of thoughts, sorting some and discarding others. As engrossed as she was, she nearly did not hear the rapid tattoo of approaching hoofbeats until too late.

Startled, she turned in her saddle, and took note of a distant dark horse and one determined rider. He was close enough, however, for her to identify the scarlet neckerchief tied about his throat and the flash of saffron waistcoat showing beneath his riding coat. That most certainly told Cat who the rider was *not*.

She also had great reason to believe that she was the sole object of his journey.

"Oh, pshaw!" she muttered. "One cannot find any peace about this place!" She quickly faced forward on her mount, glanced rapidly to the left and to the right, then straight ahead.

The descent from the ridge was a steep one, broken with the occasional jutting rock and tangle of brush. But beyond lay Lord Weyland's stables.

"We shall have some sport, then!" she murmured to her mount. With a flick of her riding crop, she went bounding down the ridge.

Chapter Four

L ord Weyland came whistling into his stables with his canine companion on his heels, a large mixed-breed hound with rough gray fur and haunches as tall as his lordship's thigh. Jack continued his cheerful rendering of a drinking song as the hound rushed ahead into the shadowed bowels of the stable, came to a dead stop in front of a stall, and drowned Jack out with his barking.

"Boofus! I say, let us hear ourselves, shall we?" Jack approached his dog. Boofus, rigid and quivering with excitement, his eyes pinned on whatever poor creature he had cornered, gave no note he had heard Jack at all.

"Oh, stop that, for heaven's sake!" A feminine voice rose above the din. "Come, you atrocious mutt! Have done!"

To Jack's surprise, Boofus silenced and lowered his head meekly. A graceful gloved hand extended from the tall box stall and permitted Boofus a sniff.

Jack walked to the stall and stopped. He now perceived the remainder of the dog-taming female, who stood with her back against the board side of the enclosure, holding the reins of her jittery mare. Her gown was rumpled and specked with straw; her bonnet was charmingly askew; her expression was purposefully serene. He struggled to suppress a smile.

"Good Lord, Boofus," he said. "It is none other than Miss D'Eauville, the Marital Prize."

Miss D'Eauville calmly adjusted her bonnet, and as she began to step forward around the anxious horse, deigned to take Jack's extended hand.

"Do not consider yourself at an advantage," she said as she stepped out of the box. As quick as that, her warm, slender hand was gone from his grip, and she was sweeping bits of straw and chaff from her skirt. "It is only accidental that I chose your stable to hide within."

Jack pursed his lips. "You were not inspecting it?"

Miss D'Eauville looked up at him then, skewering him with her incomparable brown eyes. She lifted a brow. "Hardly, Lord Weyland. Is that ridiculous man gone?"

"Which one, if I may ask?" Jack was never truly bored, for he was by nature such an inquisitive fellow— but a degree of excitement added interest to an otherwise lovely yet unremarkable morning. He prepared to fence with Miss D'Eauville.

"There is only one, other than yourself. The one in the painfully yellow waistcoat."

"Oh. *That* ridiculous man. I presume we are speaking of the one who so recently rode into my stable yard, demanded to know if I had seen Miss D'Eauville, and rode off again in a devil of a hurry. Lord Swain, I believe."

"That is the one."

She gazed up at him, one hand idly patting an adoring Boofus on the head. Somehow, Jack could not consider Boofus a traitor. He and Boofus had like minds.

"And . . . ?" she added.

He did not miss the light of amusement that was now only partially hidden in her eyes. Miss D'Eauville enjoyed the parry and thrust fully as much as he did.

"I sent the gentleman on his way. It should not have done to tell him I had Miss D'Eauville snug and tight in my stable, ready to receive my blandishments of love.''

With that, she closed her eyes and tipped her head back, giving in to a thoroughly unladylike, completely natural laugh. Boofus, confused, jumped away, and the mare shambled sideways.

"I am mortified—injured to the quick," Jack said. "I was about to add that had I known the incomparable Miss D'Eauville was in my stable, I should have run the young jackanapes off with a hay fork, and come upon you in a fervor of blandishments.''

Miss D'Eauville doubled over with laughter, and it was a moment before she could speak. Jack was treated to the delightful vision of his incomparable in the throes of unbridled and unladylike emotion.

"I am so sorry, Lord Weyland." She dabbed her eyes, clinging to the nervous mare's reins with her other hand. "I took myself upon a private morning ride, and if that wretched schoolboy Lord Swain did not spy me and decide to follow! I do *wish* this foolishness were done with." She dropped her hand from her face, and at that moment spotted something beyond Jack's shoulder. Her expression changed to one of surprise—then displeasure.

"You! So it was *you* who told Lord Swain my direction! And for what reason did you follow me, if I may ask?''

Jack turned and saw his stable boy staring helplessly at Miss D'Eauville.

"I-I beg pardon, ma'am," stammered the boy.

Jack looked back at Miss D'Eauville, who still had the boy fixed in her admonishing gaze.

"Thomas has been here all morning," Jack said.

She looked quickly back at Jack. "That cannot be! He works for Charles. This very morning he saddled my horse! I could not mistake hair as red as that!"

"My dear Miss D'Eauville, you saw Timothy. Thomas is his twin brother, and in my employ."

Miss D'Eauville's lips parted, but only for the briefest moment. "Oh. I see." She turned to the boy. "I beg your pardon, Thomas. I was mistaken."

Thomas shuffled a foot, blushing furiously. "T'ain't nothin,' ma'am."

"The boys are rather used to the confusion," Jack said mildly. "And I believe they rather enjoy it. Thomas once worked for Charles, until it seemed the twins would do better apart for all the mischief they caused." He extended his arm to Miss D'Eauville, and without hesitation she slipped her hand into the crook of his elbow. "Thomas, will you attend Miss D'Eauville's horse, please?

"The odd thing about the boys," he said as they walked toward the open doorway to the stable yard, "is that they seem to know what the other is thinking. A curious puzzle, is it not? Even now, Thomas and Timothy are likely plotting together, as much as they are two miles distant."

"You jest," Miss D'Eauville said archly. "And do not think you may distract me. Where do you intend to take me?"

"Into my house, of course."

"I think that would not be proper, even for me. A ridiculous thing, but there it is."

"Ah, but my aunt is in the house. Unless you would have her come to the stables?" He spoke, of course, as though this were a real proposal.

She responded in kind. "Oh, in that case, I shall come. I think she might gain a rather mistaken impression of me, otherwise."

"Very good."

"And just why," said Miss D'Eauville as they stepped into the sunshine, "are you at home? I had thought you at Lord Ralston's."

"Then you made an erroneous presumption. I have my own warm bed but a short ride away. Why should I not sleep in it?"

"One generally sleeps at one's host's home."

"And then one takes an early morning ride to escape the lot of the guests."

She laughed. He enjoyed her laugh. It seemed every time he heard it, he was reminded anew just how much.

"I understand now," she said. "But your case is scarcely as hard as mine; you are not expected to marry one of them."

His urge to smile vanished like the bee around the distant garden wall. He walked beside her, smelling her soft jasmine scent, feeling her dainty hand upon his arm and the rhythmic yet graceful strength of her step; and he thought that no, he was not expected to marry one of them—particularly, not this one. And he found the thought a surprisingly sad one.

"Good heavens, Jack, whatever has happened to her?"

The pretty woman in apron and cap gazed at Cat in consternation, and Cat discerned that this lady was not the housekeeper who had come to the door, in spite of her serviceable round gown and smock. She was tall and slim, her soft face scarcely lined, and she was obviously on familiar terms with the lord of the manor.

"I found her in the stables, Aunt." Lord Weyland led Cat into the front hall, and she glanced covertly at him to make out his expression. Deadpan. One could not guess the humorous vein of his answer if one did not know him as she did. And she guessed she knew him as well—nay, better—than many.

"Do not tell me such rubbish," said his aunt. She turned to Cat. "You must not pay attention to all he says. He has still a prankster inside him, all of ten years old."

Cat hardly knew whether to laugh or keep still. She smiled instead.

"My aunt, Miss Southrop," Lord Weyland said.

Miss Southrop nodded. "How do you do, Miss D'Eauville?"

So her reputation had preceded her. The teller of tales could be none other than Lord Weyland; Cat wondered precisely what he had told his aunt of her.

"I am quite well, thank you."

"We must have some tea and refreshments." Miss Southrop turned to a mobcapped maid, who had appeared at her side. "Mary—have Bates bring us our tea. We shall be in the morning room."

Miss Southrop turned and led the way before Cat could offer any explanation for her presence, or receive any query about it. It was a matter for musing. But as Miss Southrop preceded them down the hall of polished parquet wainscoting and gleaming marble tile, punctuated by beautifully maintained Louis XIV chairs and inlaid side tables, Cat's thoughts went in another direction. She looked up. The ornate plasterwork ceiling high overhead was free of cobwebs. The brocade drapes she glimpsed in the room they passed showed no signs of fading. The silver wall sconces were mirror-polished. As with the outside of the manor, she saw not a single thing that bespoke limited funds or neglect.

"Here we are. Right this way. I love this room in the morning. You can look out at the garden and see so many birds! Of course, Jack loves his birds. I suppose he has told you about it."

Miss Southrop directed Cat to a pretty blue velvet settee that faced the wide French windows and took the chair nearest her. Lord Weyland sat on her opposite hand.

"I have heard nothing of birds as yet," said Cat. "I should love to, however." Her gaze took in a pretty inlaid rosewood occasional table before them, the Aubusson carpet in reds and blues beneath their feet, the polished and dusted pianoforte in the corner, and finally the stately windows that looked out upon a vast and picturesque garden.

The English had such a way with gardens, she thought. Charles's garden was excellent; but more, Lord

Weyland's was lovely, with its formal bones yet wildish air. There were indeed many birds, flitting about and occupying the variety of shrubs and trees, and none were precisely like the ones she saw at home. She leaned forward in her chair, entranced.

"What kinds of birds do you have? Do they sing? Oh, what is that with the white on top of his head?"

Miss Southrop laughed. "So like your father! So full of curiosity."

Cat looked inquiringly at Jack, whose expression said nothing, then at Miss Southrop. "You are acquainted with my father?"

Miss Southrop's lips parted, and for a second she hesitated. Then she smiled. "I was long ago. I lived here then, you see. I had come to stay with my sister, Jack's mother."

Cat felt a rush of delight at the discovery. Here was someone who had known her father *then*, someone who had seen him as a young man and heard his youthful words.

"You must tell me all about how things were then. Father would prose on and on about the hunting and such like, but never say anything of real interest! What was Father like?"

Miss Southrop blinked. "Let me think. I recall him to be a very tall, well-favored young man, full of dash and pluck, and very much admired. But he was not the heir, and so left to seek his fortune, much to the sorrow of the ladies." She paused. "I was, of course, quite young then, and can say little more. But you must tell me about your family. Have you brothers or sisters? And how is your father?"

Cat was disappointed at Miss Southrop's unsatisfactory answer. She wanted to pursue her question further, but sensed that patience was the wisest course.

"Oh, I am afraid I am Father's only child. But Father is extremely well. Full of vigor, full of ideas. He is thinking of a new business now."

"He was forever making plans. I think he has not changed so very much. I must admit, I did not expect his daughter to be so very like." Miss Southrop fell silent, and Cat sensed she had fallen into solitary thought.

Cat's gaze strayed to where Lord Weyland was now standing near the French windows, looking out. She saw that he was watching a reddish-brown bird flit from branch to branch in the box hedge.

Lord Weyland must have realized his aunt had known her father. How odd, Cat thought, that he had never mentioned it.

"It is so lovely here," Cat said. "I sometimes wonder how Father could leave, but of course, he had no choice."

Whatever answer she hoped to prompt was never given, for at that moment a manservant arrived with the tea tray. He wore a very proper coat, a spotless neckerchief, and knee breeches without a sign of wear; his stockings had not been darned, and his shoes were highly polished. With perfect demeanor he placed the tray on the table and withdrew.

Cat remembered her earlier thoughts. Lord Weyland's home hardly appeared to be that of an impoverished peer. He had not prepared for visitors, and yet the rooms she had seen were well furnished and spotless. At the very least he kept adequate servants—and expensive male servants, no less. Her unpleasant suspicion grew.

"You seem quite comfortable here," Cat said. She deliberately addressed herself to Lord Weyland's aunt.

Miss Southrop poured the tea, not looking up. "We are. My family left me little more than my pride. I count myself fortunate that I have my nephew to look after me. My father claimed bad luck, but my Jack is very clever about investments and such things."

"How terrible!"

"Goodness, how is it terrible?" Miss Southrop stopped

in the act of passing Cat's cup of tea, looking bewildered. "I am very fortunate to have such care."

"Oh—I mean, how wonderful!" Cat reached for the cup of tea. What in the devil had got into her? Lord Weyland was *still* only a baron—he might as well have money. It made no difference to her if he was not poor—he was not on The List.

Miss Southrop gazed over her cup at Cat. "Yes, my Jack is quite the marital catch, although as yet he will have none of it. He shall quite force me to desperate measures."

"Aunt, I believe Miss D'Eauville asked about flowers."

Cat met Lord Weyland's gaze. He stood yet by the windows, only now he was looking at her. There was something inscrutable in his eyes.

"You must take a walk in the garden," Miss Southrop was saying. "I am sure Lord Weyland would be happy to escort you. The roses are coming out, and they are delightful."

The air seemed to crackle between herself and Lord Weyland, and Cat felt as though there were no one in the room but themselves. His gaze seemed to go deeper, truer than it ever had before, and Cat felt . . . confused.

Cat sensed that at this precise moment, walking in the garden with Lord Weyland was not wise. But all she could think of was their similar tour of Charles's garden, and how Lord Weyland had made her laugh, and how she had felt light and happy and . . . warm, just as she felt now. Had her heart sped up then, too? Yes, she thought it had. These feelings, she thought, were not the feelings she should be having for a man she would not marry.

But she had them, nevertheless.

Walking in the garden with Lord Weyland was not a good plan.

"I think I should be returning home before I am wondered about," Cat said. "Lord Ralston may get into one of his dithers. Another time, I would love to see the garden."

Was it relief she felt from Lord Weyland . . . or was he sorry? But perhaps she was only sensing her own emotions.

"I shall ride back with you," he said. "We shall take Thomas, and all will believe you rode out with Timothy."

"You rode without an escort?" exclaimed Miss Southrop. For a moment, Cat thought a reprimand was forthcoming, but surprisingly, none came.

"Well, it is no matter now that Jack is at hand to work it all out," Miss Southrop said. "My nephew is a very clever man."

"I believe you told me," said Lord Weyland, "that my fortune did not matter."

Cat rode beside Lord Weyland, gazing straight ahead, taking care to keep her mare from the reach of his testy gelding. Lord Weyland's dry, knowing voice gave her a case of prickles. It was like having velvet rubbed against the back of one's neck.

"But I do like to have a correct grasp of the essential facts, Lord Weyland. You *did* allow me to think wrongly."

"Well, then, I apologize for giving you that misapprehension. The sad truth is that I have a rather nicely feathered nest, clever man that I am. But I assure you, Miss D'Eauville, I neither sleep on rose petals nor bathe in wine, nor do I keep an exotic beauty in the local inn."

"Very well. I accept your apology. But only because you do not waste perfectly good wine."

In reality, Cat knew she had simply believed as she had wished about Lord Weyland, and it was not his duty to correct her. And she also forgave him because she liked his company so much, and would never give it up over a trifle. But what did this mean? She felt him now as he rode beside her on his giant gelding, all controlled strength, easy grace, and blade-sharp penetration. She could think of no other man that she was so very *aware* of.

Drat him!

"Ah, my conscience smites me," he said. "I confess I do play piquet with my aunt. She is a sorceress at cards, and occasionally lightens my pocket. I daresay my mother's side of the family is where my cleverness comes from."

"But not your purse, I gather. Now that is the thing that always puzzles me. Women must forever be at the mercy of foolish men, when they could manage their fortunes so much better themselves. I grant that you may be the exception, Lord Weyland, but in general, it is a ridiculous thing." She fastened her gaze at a distant hillock, and noted that a hawk circled in the blue overhead. It was now late morning, and a trifle less cool than earlier, and she should be enjoying her ride home. But something was needling at her.

"I presume your good father controls your purse?"

"That is neither here nor there. We are speaking of you."

"Being that I am not on your list, Miss D'Eauville, might I inquire how my financial status interests you?"

She felt his look and knew he had tossed her a challenge. She attempted to rise to it.

"It doesn't at all. I simply do not like to be mistaken." She looked at him and smiled. "Do you?"

His handsome English face remained blank. "No. Which puts me in mind of your present endeavor. What do you think of your gallants?"

She studied his calm face in profile, and determined that much stirred beneath the surface; and she knew she must keep on her toes. "As yet, I am not overthrown with delight."

"Ah. Now, let us see. What of our Lord Macclesby?" His tone was offhand, but she sensed interest.

"Conceited and boring. I would certainly have to travel if I married him, or I should lose my mind."

"I see you have not recognized a very important characteristic in the gentleman. He likes to have his way. He will not, if he can at all prevail, allow someone else to have the upper hand."

She gave him an arch look. "How can you know this?"

He continued to gaze straight ahead, calmly guiding his mount. "Simple observation. His behavior, manner of talking, his fastidiousness. I also noted he is quickly moved to anger."

"You cannot know that."

"I can. A man notices this about other men. If he can not, he is likely to come to grief—or fisticuffs, at the very least."

"How interesting. I find it amazing that in a civilized society, gentlemen must consider such things."

"Gentlemen are still gentle*men*, Miss D'Eauville, for better or for worse." He shot her a glance. "One can send them to the best tailor and teach them to dance, but in their deepest hearts, they prefer a mill to a minuet."

"What a clever way of putting it. Do you like a mill, Lord Weyland?"

She was enjoying herself again. Disappointments never depressed her spirits for long; and moreover, it was much easier to keep the acquaintance of a wealthy man than a poor one. And she *did* wish to keep Lord Weyland's acquaintance.

Purse strings or heartstrings—none of hers were entangled. No, certainly not. She was a woman of rare resolve.

"I am a very logical man, Miss D'Eauville. I never allow emotion to overtake my reason."

"How very lofty of you. I stand much impressed, indeed."

She caught a quiver at the corner of his lips, which he quickly suppressed.

"Miss D'Eauville, you are being very clever, but not

clever enough. We are discussing your beaux. Now, what of Lord Rhodes?"

Cat thought of the older gentleman with his unprepossessing appearance and modest, albeit morose, demeanor. "He is a very good man, I believe. He is settled and appears to be the sort who likes to please. He should do, I suppose, but I should need to be *vastly* entertained by a gentleman to whose children I must immediately become stepmother. I am afraid he does not entertain me so very much."

"Hm. And our young Lord Swain?"

Cat grinned at Lord Weyland, whose face remained composed. "He is rather eager, is he not? And so young! One wants to pull his ears and thrust him into the schoolroom."

"One might be better served in determining if that is indeed where he belongs."

"What an odd idea! Lord Swain is one and twenty, I believe."

"Has Lord Ralston met him before?"

Cat frowned at him, then looked ahead. "I do not know. But I think perhaps you inquire *too* much, Lord Weyland."

They reached the verge of trimmed grass at the edge of Lord Ralston's property, and espied a group of persons taking refreshments alfresco beneath a large canopy. Cat sighed. Her duty lay before her, and pleasure was done.

"I see new combatants have arrived," said Lord Weyland. "Prepare to do battle, my dear."

Cat laughed. "I shall finesse them all—and that includes you, my clever, *logical* gentleman!"

She sprang her mare and left him behind with Thomas the twin, and made a spectacular sweep by the picnickers on the way to the stable.

He didn't follow her. He watched her go, with Thomas trailing her on his pony, and knew that Timothy would be waiting for them. Thomas would then slip artfully out of the stable and make his way home, and the sensational Miss Catherine D'Eauville's reputation would be spared.

When she vanished from sight, he scanned the grouping on the lawn. He recognized several of Miss D'Eauville's new prospects. A feeling stole over him that he did not wish to admit, even to himself. He wondered which would win the exceptional Miss D'Eauville.

Quite possibly, the pesky feeling was jealousy.

Chapter Five

*H*is gelding shifted impatiently beneath him. Jack decided that he, too, was tired of watching the guests mingle alfresco on Charles's lawn, but before he could rein his horse about, he was summoned.

"Jack!"

Jack saw the portly form of his childhood friend making his way toward him. For a fleeting moment, he wondered if Miss D'Eauville's arrival with him had been noticed after all.

"Hallo, Charles. I see your house is filling up."

"Yes, and that isn't the whole of it." Charles stopped next to him, removed his hat, and swiped his sweating brow. "Glad to see you. I'd like some words. Can you come to my study?"

"Now?"

"Yes. Where is that groom?" Charles slapped his hat back upon his head and turned. "Robert! Come here at once and take Lord Weyland's horse!"

Jack dismounted and handed his reins to the servant. "It sounds grave."

"It could be mine," Charles said mournfully. "Come."

Moments later Jack followed Charles into Charles's study. There, Jack was surprised to see another gentleman waiting for them, a stranger, standing by the hearth with a funeral expression on his face.

"Lord Swain, I should like you to meet my trusted friend and adviser, Lord Weyland."

Jack extended his hand and shook the one presented to him by the new Lord Swain. "Pleased to meet you. Might I then surmise that the Lord Swain I have had the pleasure of knowing is not whom he presents himself to be?"

Lord Swain nodded grimly. "I am deeply sorry, but my young brother absconded with my invitation to this function. I admit I gave it no important thought at first, but then my mother informed me that the American cousin who was to be honored is unwed and seeking a titled husband. I of course set forth for Ralston immediately."

"The young man who was in our midst was not Swain," Charles inserted, "but Mr. Harry Swain. This is the most devilish thing. We have already sent him packing—Swain arrived early this morning, and young Harry returned from his ride not long after. Weyland, I need your counsel."

"Harry is but seventeen," Swain interjected. "I have recently formed a beneficial engagement, but my brother is not so well set. He has lately been sent down from Eton, and I have been attempting to guide him. Clearly, I have not been successful."

"I see," said Jack.

"I want no scandal," Swain continued. "My brother will be punished enough when all is done. I shall certainly see to it that he learns a lesson from this."

"I believe Charles is of the same mind," Jack replied. "We must of course advise Miss D'Eauville, but you may trust her discretion."

Charles sucked in a breath. "Jack, I do not think that would be—"

"We may trust her discretion," Jack repeated, giving Charles a firm look. "She should be summoned immediately."

Charles gave the point, and the butler was sent for

and promptly dispatched in search of Miss D'Eauville.
Jack hoped she had successfully arrived in the house.
Certainly, her early morning ride could have pro-
voked questions.

Miss D'Eauville could not be brought right away. She
had must needs change after her ride, it seemed, being
in no mind of a meeting without being properly dressed
for the occasion. The conversation between the men
lagged, and eventually pursued the health of Swain's
mother, the status of his in-laws, the taxes upon
window-glazing and the state of the roads before the
butler opened the door and presented Miss D'Eauville
to the room.

She was dressed in a lovely gown of blue-striped
muslin, a matching blue ribbon laced about her upswept hair, and a string of coral beads. A smile danced
upon her lips, and she extended a gloved and beringed
hand for the gentlemen to do homage to.

"Here I am! I am so sorry to keep you gentlemen
waiting. I have had a very busy morning. My dear
Charl—Lord Ralston, pray present me."

Ralston cleared his throat. "Weyland?"

Jack smiled and stepped forward to accept her hand,
then bowed properly over it. "Miss D'Eauville, it appears that the pleasure falls to me. Let me introduce
Lord Swain . . . the proper Lord Swain, as it were."

Miss D'Eauville's eyes widened slightly. Then, in a
flash, her smile returned, an amused quirk at one corner
of her lips.

"Lord Swain? I sense some explanation is forthcoming."

Swain stepped forward and took his turn at proper
greeting. "My dear Miss D'Eauville, you are quite correct. My younger brother is the masquerader, and I pray
you forgive him. He is barely more than a boy. He has
been sent away from here with a severe reprimand, and
you may be sure that he will suffer the consequences
of his actions."

"Oh, do not be too hard upon him. He seemed such a nice young man, and I am very sure he is sorry."

"As am I. I deeply regret the inconvenience and . . . embarrassment this must have caused you." He bowed his head once more and relinquished her hand. "Thank you so very much for your kind understanding. I shall now leave you to your cousin's counsel."

"Oh, but you must stay! Clearly the invitation was meant for you, and you are no less welcome." Miss D'Eauville smiled again charmingly.

"He would stay, I am sure," Jack said, "but his family, and the future Lady Swain, will be waiting for his return."

Jack watched as Miss D'Eauville turned her look upon him, then, a guarded question in her eyes. The questioning look rapidly turned to one of comprehension.

"Lord Weyland is quite right," Lord Swain said, his complexion darkening slightly. "I must bid you good day."

Jack had to give Miss D'Eauville credit. She gave her farewell to Lord Swain with perfect good manners and ease, and it was not until that gentleman had departed the room and she turned to Charles and Jack that the flash of warning came to her eyes.

"Thank you for your assistance, gentlemen," she said directly. "But I of course had concluded that the erstwhile Lord Swain would not do."

"Cousin, there are dangers to consider here. Matters must be much better thought out. One has to fear not only another impostor, but—"

"Dear me, Charles, but you do grow more trying with age! And as for you, Lord Weyland, I do not wish one wise word from you. I go on very well without either of you."

Miss D'Eauville turned on her heel, and Jack honored her request, letting her depart the room in silence.

On the heels of Miss D'Eauville's departure, Jack

went to the sideboard, took up a crystal decanter and a glass, and began to pour.

"Fortification, Ralston?"

"Yes, and hurry, dear fellow, or this headache will have the better of me."

Jack handed the full glass to Charles, then poured one for himself. Finally, he relaxed in his usual overstuffed armchair, stretched out his long legs, and crossed them at the ankle.

"Very well, Charles, what is all the fuss about?"

"What is it all about? How can you ask such a question?" Charles sat heavily, and with shoulders slumped, contemplated Jack with a frown punctuating his ruddy forehead.

"The impostor was discovered, and all is well with the world—or, at least, with Miss D'Eauville. What other problem is there? All is well that ends well, is it not?" Jack sipped, watching Charles from over the rim of his glass.

Charles sighed and leaned back. "Jack, if it were that absurdly simple, why would I ask for you? It is the whole circus of finding her a husband."

Jack held Charles's gaze. "Go on."

Charles mopped his forehead with a kerchief. "This thing is no easy matter. I have been required to invite near strangers here, Jack, solely on merit of their title and desperation for a wealthy wife. It shall be the death of me, all the hounding about and fuss and confusion. And they are eating and drinking me out of a small fortune, by gad! The more they owe, the more they eat. And you know that I can't afford it! I wish I'd never told my uncle I would do this."

"You saw your duty. It is to your credit. But if it comes to that, I believe Miss D'Eauville could manage the thing very well by herself. She certainly seems capable of it. Were you aware of her list?"

"That." Charles waved a hand dismissively. "She is determined to do it her way, and she is damned particular. She wrote to my sainted wife for months compiling that thing. She would have nothing less than getting the lot of them here so she could pick and choose! It isn't the way such a thing should be done!"

"I should think the eliminations have already begun."

Charles sighed. "Yes, I am sure they have. But I have known her since she was a child, and she has her own mind. She might up and decide to marry some commoner if he suited her fancy! Or another damned impostor who might be here in our very midst! And then where would I be?"

Jack raised his brows and gently swirled his glass. "Where would you be?"

"Done up, that's where."

"They shan't eat that much. Touch me if you need to. You know I'm willing to help."

Charles swore. "I bloody will not! That is preposterous! And anyway, all I have to do is pull this thing off, and I'll be set. It just has me worried, that's all."

Jack felt a chill of foreboding. "How will you be set?"

Charles heaved a sigh. Then he stood, walked slowly to the south window, and clasped his hands behind him. From there, he had a clear view of the stables, but Jack could see that Charles was not preoccupied with the scenery.

"Her father made a bargain with me. If I bring about a good match for his daughter, he will pay me ten thousand pounds."

Damn. Jack stared at his friend, and thought it again. *Damn.*

"She must not know." Charles turned back to face Jack. "Miss D'Eauville. She does not know, and her father does not want her to know. It is between him and me."

It was Jack's turn to sigh. Still mentally off balance from Charles's revelation, he sought to answer. "Then you must do the thing rightly. That is all."

"Gad, don't I know! But I can't control this pack of

fortune hunters, Jack, much less her! I hardly know how I will manage!" He paused. "I need your help. You can handle this sort of thing. You can guide her. I know you can."

Jack gazed at the woebegone face of his oldest friend, and his heart ached. Charles had needed his help on occasions past . . . but this was more than he'd ever asked before. Charles did not understand that, of course. Only Jack knew how painful this help would be. And Jack hadn't fully realized it himself, until now. How was it that he realized how very much he wished not to lose something, only when it was plain he must?

But he couldn't let his old friend down.

"I'll see what I can do."

Charles's worried face broke into a smile. "I knew you would do it. You are a true friend. I owe you more than I can ever repay."

Indeed he would. "It should be easy enough." Jack drained his glass of sherry. "I believe your cousin has a liking for me . . . and I do believe I am as clever as she is. She is as good as wed to a duke—or an earl at least."

"Splendid! Let us drink to it then!" Charles went to the sideboard and retrieved the decanter.

"Yes. Let us drink to Miss D'Eauville . . . and her future felicity." Jack held out his newly emptied glass. The drink, at least, was a pleasant prospect.

"As you are mentioning him, Becky, would you so kindly draw a line through his name? I would do it, but you have not your dress on yet, and ink raises the very devil with silk."

Cat, seated at her dressing table, continued fussing with the clasp of a diamond necklet that was surely worth more than the fortunes of many of the guests awaiting her grand arrival in the ballroom downstairs. The casement window was open to the warmish summer breeze, and Becky sat before it in Cat's window seat, still in her dressing gown, having come purpose-fully to Cat's chamber for a serious discussion. Cat, however, was not so desirous of a conversation as Becky. Becky had a way of complicating things merely by thinking about them.

"I do not think The List is of principal importance at the moment," Becky said. "The young man has been taken away, a discovered impostor. You must have more to say than 'draw a line through his name.' "

"What else is there to be done?" Cat fumbled at the back of her neck. "This dratted thing! Becky, since you are here, can you please help fasten this?"

"I could call your maid," Becky said, but she arose and came to the back of Cat's chair. Fastening the necklace, Becky said to the back of Cat's head, "The fact that you have been courted by an impostor should raise a modicum of alarm. There could well be others as desperate. I think we should review our strategy and take steps that such a thing cannot hap-pen again."

"Of course we should," Cat said. She raised her head and gazed at her reflection in the vanity mirror, as-sessing her own and Becky's handiwork. Her dark hair was upswept, with pearls threaded through; her gown of pale yellow silk was off her shoulders and cut low, and the diamonds twinkled above her queenly bosom. Cat turned her head to this angle, then that, assessing her battle-worthiness. "Becky, I leave it to you. You are so talented with those details. But I must say that there is no worry whatsoever, for I would never choose an impostor. I would make very certain of a gentleman's qualifications before taking any fatal step, you can de-pend upon it!"

"You were perhaps believing that Lord—that young Mr. Swain was the person he said he was. You would have had no reason to believe otherwise, as Lord Ral-ston invited him to this house."

"You worry overly much. I would have made certain."

Cat rose, moved gracefully around Becky, and stopped before the cheval glass. She turned slowly before it, giving herself a final assessment. Becky's reflection was an unfocused shadow behind her.

"In any case, Becky, I had already determined that Lord—that Mr. Swain was too young and would not suit."

"What of the others, then?"

Cat turned to face Becky. Her cousin and oldest friend was being more persistent than usual this time, and she focused her attention.

"Lord Macclesby is too pompous and dull, and Lord Weyland believes he may not be so very tractable."

Becky raised her brows, standing as primly as ever with her hands clasped before her. "Lord Weyland believes . . . ?"

Cat stared into Becky's questioning eyes. "He offered advice. He is quite clever, although he is not *always* correct, of course. Men do have a tendency to think overly well of their own intelligence. It is best not to encourage them, so say nothing, if you please."

Something Lord Weyland had said about Mr. Swain niggled at the back of her mind. Cat frowned. It seemed Lord Weyland's judgment had been accurate. His advice might be depended upon, she thought; but besides being annoyed that she had not suspected the problem herself, she was bothered by the fact that she might have needed his assistance.

She could not afford to *need* a man, particularly one she liked so well.

"What of Lord Rhodes?" Becky asked.

Cat waved her hand dismissively. "I do not know. Perhaps he will do." Tired as she was of the questioning, she thought she caught something strange in Becky's eyes. But before she could determine what it was, it was gone, and Becky's delicate features assumed their usual serene state.

"Perhaps you should aspire to more than someone who will 'do.' There is no need to rush into marriage."

"I am not rushing. Goodness, dear, we worked long and arduously on my list! And the sooner I am married, the sooner I may go on with my life."

Becky blinked. "Then I shall return to my room and cross Lord Swain off The List. And then I shall dress, for we should not wish to be late tonight."

"Of course we should," Cat said. "Silly girl! If there was ever a time a woman should not appear eager, not that she ever should, mind you—it is not upon the night she means to select a husband."

Cat watched as Becky exited the chamber. Then Cat sank down on her dressing table chair and continued to stare at the closed door.

"Piffle," she said out loud. Her thoughts tumbled about and made a thorough confusion of themselves. It was not at all how she liked to be, and something she was not used to.

She had not joined the guests that afternoon. Instead, she had claimed indisposition—falsely, of course—and spent the time writing her father a letter in her room. She had assured herself that she did so as there was great value in increasing the anticipation of her beaux, and the time in solitude strengthened her for the evening to come. But it also had the perverse effect of making her think.

The time had come to fulfill her father's wishes and choose a noble husband—but while it had begun as but a step in her planned life's journey that seemed the better for completion, now she felt the time was too soon. She was unprepared to marry, whereas she once had believed she was fully ready to acquire the husband of her father's dreams. But that had been when her dreams and her father's did not argue with each other.

She hoped that Becky had not guessed. Her odd emotions were too new, and she was determined that they must be wrong.

"Nothing has changed," she said aloud, again to herself. Her plan was no different. She wanted to—she *must*—marry, which would then allow her to continue to do as she liked. She only needed to find the right gentleman.

Her father had always said that his Cat had the mind of a good soldier. She could size up her circumstances, determine a strategy, and force all distractions from her thoughts. Tonight she was about increasing her worth to her assembled court, and her very careful toilette—her décolletage as well as her diamond necklet—were very much part of her plan.

She also intended to make matters clear. She was no demure, submissive thing wanting a master—she *was* her own mistress, and would remain so.

Her future was too large a stake to treat carelessly.

Lord Weyland's clever winsome face appeared in her mind, and she felt another uncomfortable twinge. Could not Lord Weyland be part of "doing as she liked" once the business of marriage was done? But no, she thought not, for she suspected matters would not remain simple. Lord Weyland did not seem the sort of gentleman to blindly comply with her wishes, which in this case, was to play her tame beau for as long as she desired. And how terrible that sounded! She would not desire such an arrangement for herself, should matters be reversed. As would Lord Weyland, she would wish him well in his married life, a cheery Godspeed, and go about her business.

How she wished this venture did not necessitate the losing of a friend!

The American Heiress was not going to be prompt, Jack observed. He smiled to himself and gazed about the interesting gathering in the Ralston drawing room. It was a large enough room with the furniture moved aside, but with the doors open to the hall as were the doors to the Blue Salon opposite, there was plenty of room for the guests to mix and mingle. He himself stood near the open doors to the hallway, a position where he might view new arrivals as well as those entering the salon across the way.

The male dinner guests were all accounted for, with the exception of several married gentlemen who had departed to the billiards room. Charles, of course, was here, looking red-faced and nervous, striding among the guests and engaging in snatches of conversation. He, like Jack, was awaiting the arrival of Miss D'Eauville.

There was a nice contingent of females as well, Jack saw, but it would be rather awkward if there were not. One did have to balance the numbers, and of course Charles's wife would see to that. Jack was happy to have his own aunt among the number; his dear Aunt Bea saw far too little of society, and he had feared she would seek an excuse for this night. Rather surprisingly, she had not. She was at this moment in conversation with Charles's wife and a circle of friends.

Although Miss D'Eauville was not yet down, her American cousin, Miss Prescott, had a time ago arrived and was now conversing with Lord Rhodes. Miss Prescott, Jack had decided, was the managing sort, with a keen but maternal eye; she appeared content to follow in Miss D'Eauville's wake, an unacknowledged protector, but her observation clearly extended to matters beyond her cousin's affairs. Lord Rhodes had been alone and appearing rather desolate until Miss Prescott had arrived. Most assuredly, she had perceived his condition and assumed a mission of mercy. Unless, of course, she meant to engage his attention away from Miss D'Eauville. . . .

An interesting relationship between the two cousins, Jack thought. He would record his ideas on that. Where Miss D'Eauville inspired, Miss Prescott calmed. Where Miss D'Eauville would be gay and impulsive, Miss

Prescott would watch and weigh with a serene yet critical eye. Miss D'Eauville shone like a beacon, while Miss Prescott cast a cool shadow, unnoticed and faithful to a fault.

"Jack, I say, where has she got to? Everyone is as nervous as a cat at a fireworks display. I *wish* my cousin would display a little more concern for the convenience of others!"

Jack turned to Charles, who stood by tugging at his neckcloth with one finger and looking as uncomfortable as a substantial man could at a warm affair.

"Have you asked Miss Prescott where she is?"

"Yes. She said that Miss D'Eauville would be down presently. Presently! That could be at any time at all! It could be at cock's crow for all we know!"

"True," said Jack. He gazed casually around them. At the moment they were able to speak in relative privacy; Charles would have ascertained that, but Jack felt it always wise to be sure. "I trust that this is a stratagem, Charles, and you can leave matters to Miss D'Eauville with an easy mind."

"*Your* mind may be easy, but you may be sure that *mine* is not. You should consider yourself fortunate not to have a cousin like Miss D'Eauville!"

"But I do. There are times when being of different blood bears a distinct advantage."

Charles huffed. "I hope you are not thinking of marrying her. Of course, even cousins may do that, not that I would ever have considered such a thing!"

"No, I am not thinking of marrying her."

"I know you aren't. I know you too well, Jack. You would as soon dance arse-naked for the queen as marry."

"No, I should *prefer* to dance arse-naked for the queen."

"There, then. We understand each other very well."

It was then that Jack caught a flash of pale yellow in the corner of his eye—at a startlingly near proximity, at that. Of course Miss D'Eauville would choose that precise moment to arrive.

He turned and gave her a gentlemanly nod. "Miss D'Eauville."

She looked absolutely ravishing. There was nothing like the gloriously shapely, statuesquely dazzling Miss D'Eauville in a gown of yellow silk, and then there was so much bosom to be admired. And yet, all seemed overshadowed by her lively face and twinkling brown eyes. They twinkled, in fact, a good deal more than usual.

No, there was little chance she had not heard his last remark.

She extended her hand, graceful as a queen herself. "Lord Weyland . . . and my dear cousin Lord Ralston. What a lovely affair this appears to be. I am nearly overwhelmed by the grandeur of it all."

Jack took her hand and bowed over it, brushing her glove with his lips. He returned his gaze to her eyes, and saw the mischief there.

"I declare," she said, "this is almost as exciting as meeting the Queen of England."

Touché.

"Catherine," Charles sputtered under his breath. "Miss D'Eauville, *please.*"

Clearly Charles perceived the dangerous possibilities here. Jack could not help but smile.

"Do you not think it would be *more* exciting to meet the queen?" Jack asked.

Miss D'Eauville arched a brow. "More exciting? If I were to meet her alone, I do not know. But I do believe it would be if you were to accompany me, Lord Weyland."

"Miss D'Eauville," Charles said sharply, "there are several new guests eager to meet you. Shall we proceed?"

"Of course, cousin." She transferred her hand from Jack to her cousin's, and Jack felt a sharp sense of loss.

It was as though he had held a goblet of warm wine in his hand, and the warmth had made a molten path up his arm.

"Lady Ralston!" Jack heard Charles call. "Come help me present our Miss D'Eauville!"

And so the evening had begun, and Jack recalled duty. He had made a promise to Charles, a promise he intended to keep.

At least there was the advantage of watching the dazzling Miss D'Eauville go about charming every red-blooded male in the room. And if he wished to steal Miss D'Eauville for himself and kiss her senseless, it was a desire he could live with. It was the desire to marry her that he could not.

If only he preferred to dance arse-naked for the queen.

Cat proceeded across the drawing room on Lord Ralston's arm, her smile impossible to be rid of. She could not recall the last time something she had overheard had so amused her. Poor Charles's face still bore a trace of red, but although Lord Weyland had betrayed nothing in his manner and look that suggested he was embarrassed as well, Cat was certain that he had been.

So Lord Weyland had much rather not marry! That was an entirely agreeable bit of information, as well. She might laugh with him and twit him as much as she pleased, and there would be no lady friend to interfere with their pleasant relationship. Matters would only change when she herself changed them.

She was still smiling when Charles delivered her to his wife for introductions, and it was with surprising delight that she saw Lord Weyland's aunt at her side. Miss Southrop's eyes sparkled, and she extended her hand.

"My dear Miss D'Eauville! It is a pleasure indeed."

Cat was amused that Lord Weyland's aunt did not mention their previous meeting, pretending a first acquaintance with her. It was much as her nephew had done in the same circumstance.

Cat took Miss Southrop's hand in greeting. "You are, of course, Lord Weyland's aunt."

"I am indeed."

Miss Southrop looked, Cat thought, remarkably fine for a mature woman. She possessed a graceful figure, and wore her rose silk very well, with a pretty lace shawl over her shoulders. Then there was the brightness of her eyes, which now examined Cat with great alertness.

"I am so happy you have come. Did you not know my father?" Cat asked innocently.

Of course, Miss Southrop smiled. "I had his acquaintance. And might I say, my dear, that you are very like him. You have the D'Eauville look about you, just as he did."

Lady Ralston laughed lightly. "Lord Ralston resembles his mother rather more. Our young William has more of the D'Eauville look."

"Such a handsome man William will be," Miss Southrop said. "As is my nephew, do you not think, Miss D'Eauville?"

On that head, Cat did very much agree. On the point of response, however, Cat found herself interrupted by the arrival of a gentleman at her side.

"Ladies, I deliver my profound good wishes for the evening." Lord Macclesby bowed stiffly to Miss Southrop and Lady Ralston, then rotated on his heels and delivered a more protracted bow to Cat. "We are to have dancing, I believe. I do hope I may partner you during the evening."

"You may," said Cat.

"And if I may be so bold, I would much like to take you down to dinner."

Cat could not think that an enjoyable prospect, but she also remembered her duty. She was not, after all, seeking a marriage partner for pleasure.

"I am not taken as yet, so you may do so."

"Delightful."

"I am determined to be delighted in any event, so it is most fortunate."

Dinner was, indeed, only a tolerable affair. Cat was seated to her best advantage with Lord Macclesby on her one hand, and Lord Rhodes on her other. But while Lady Ralston's arrangements may have been for the best, Cat found no pleasure in listening to Lord Macclesby's boasts of his hunting prowess, or in the awkward silence from Lord Rhodes, who sat by an equally quiet Becky. In addition, Lord Macclesby had the unfortunate inclination to choose for her dishes she would rather not eat.

"You have certainly shot a lot of game," Cat said to him at last. "I am surprised you have any creatures left to shoot at." She prodded at the cold ham on her plate and eyed a dish of pheasant at a distance too far away for her to reach.

"There is plenty for me to shoot at," Lord Macclesby said, giving her a superior look. "I keep the strictest watch for poachers. It is the poachers that are such a very bad thing. One must not have anyone and everyone shooting on their land."

"I see." Cat gave up and attacked the ham. "Then I shall have to go to Africa."

"To Africa?

"To hunt, of course." Cat took a bite of ham and sensed Lord Macclesby's hesitation. He was clearly attempting to understand her; she wished he would, but held out little hope.

"Why should you wish to hunt in Africa?" Lord Macclesby asked. "You would of course be welcome to hunt as you liked on my land. I should be happy to guide you. It is not as though, after all, that you would kill so very much."

Cat turned to him and smiled. "I am a very fine markswoman," she said. "I shall kill your last partridge, and then where shall you be?"

Lord Macclesby blinked. "But Africa . . . you need not . . ." He paused, clearly seeing the pitfalls that lay before him.

Lord Rhodes cleared his throat. It was the first sound Cat had heard him make for a half hour. "You might shoot all of my partridges and welcome," he said quietly. "If you wished."

"Miss D'Eauville can of course kill all of my partridges," Lord Macclesby said irritably. "I should even go to Africa. In fact, I should insist upon it!"

Cat was tempted beyond all reason to wish him a pleasant journey. She took another bite of ham instead.

Would this dinner ever end? And was Lord Macclesby indeed the best she could do? Cat sent an inquiring look at her cousin Lord Ralston and failed to catch his eye. He appeared to be in animated conversation with his female neighbor, Mrs. Barbury. Near them, Cat saw Lord Weyland speaking to Miss Barbury. She wished he would look over at her. He did not.

Her gaze finally went to Miss Southrop. Lord Weyland's aunt was seated next to an Admiral Bowers, and seemed politely intent on his words. Cat wished that she had been seated near her so they might have conversed more about Cat's father. She could only hope for an opportunity later that evening.

Dinner ended at last. To Cat's annoyance, Lord Macclesby continued to stay close to her side, whether or not he had something to say, as though claiming some right to the position. Like a fly by a honey pot, Lord Macclesby had no perception that he was not wanted. Every time she turned, he was there, and it mattered not with whom she was in conversation or that she had already partnered him in dance as many times as propriety and her patience would allow.

It quite prevented her further conversation with Miss Southrop about her father, and it seemed she was not to be rescued. Lord Rhodes made rather mournful, longing looks at her but humbly kept his distance, and Lord

Weyland pursued his own conversation in another circle of guests. In addition, whenever Cat looked to Charles, he was smiling and approving, with the most benignly insensible expression on his face. Cat found herself actually missing young Mr. Swain, as much as he had tricked her and forced her to hide in Lord Weyland's stable. He was callow and passionate and impulsive, and should have been good for disturbing Lord Macclesby's pomposity.

Lord Carlisle, newly arrived, offered some respite, despite the addiction to cards alluded to by Weyland—but only until she realized he was a shorter, rounder version of Lord Macclesby. In her first dance with Lord Carlisle, she took care to tread heavily upon his foot.

"Oh, I am *so* sorry, Lord Carlisle! I cannot think how I came to be so very clumsy!" Cat stepped back from the wincing lord, finessing him from the line of the dance, and caught the eye of a footman. She signaled him with alacrity.

"Please assist Lord Carlisle to a chair, and get him a strong drink—brandy, I think. He has gone quite lame."

He left her with mixed regret and thankfulness, Cat saw with satisfaction. She turned then, and found herself gazing at the neatly tied neckcloth of another gentleman.

"Miss D'Eauville, I am beginning to think you a merciless woman."

Cat looked up at Lord Weyland's deceptively passive face and smiled, cognizant of a good deal of grateful relief. "Is that what you believe? I am injured. I am merciful in the extreme. Only think how horrid it would be for some innocent, unsuspecting gentleman to find himself joined to *me*."

"You wish for someone reprehensible and devious? I can scarcely serve you, madam, if I do not know your preferences."

Cat took note of the pure, clear gray of Lord Weyland's eyes, of the tiny laugh lines at their corners, and the very nice, firm shape of his lips with which he betrayed not a hint of a smile. An awareness tingled in her backbone, a thing she had felt before with him.

"What a foolish man you are. If my list were made up of reprehensible and devious men, I should not be bored witless. I should not have to tread on their toes."

"But, madam, those qualities would be the very reason that you *must* tread on their toes. Or ought I to go back to my breeding a superior strain of fowl and plead ignorance of the nature of man?"

"Actually, sir, I do not think the nature of man and the nature of fowl is so very different. They strut and crow and display their colors, and act very fierce when it is all a sham. A wise hen, as well as a wise woman, must penetrate the facade to protect herself. And so, you know your own answer—you cannot be of great assistance to me, for you are handicapped by your sex."

"Then I cannot help you to avoid a certain gentleman, who is approaching you quite determinedly from the rear."

Cat quickly caught Lord Weyland's wrist. "One must not rush to conclusions. You might walk with me."

"To where would you like to walk?"

"Pretend you are a cock who is running away from a fight. I am certain that would do."

Lord Weyland turned and gallantly offered his arm. In a trice he was expertly conducting her away, she supposed, from a frustrated Lord Macclesby. Indeed, a good man did have his usefulness. She glanced up at Lord Weyland's handsomely molded face, at once so stately and disguising such humor, and felt a small thrill . . . of delight, or happiness, or even of contentment. How could she feel this for a man of whom common sense dictated she should discourage? A man who was not on her list?

And what would her father think of that?

Chapter Six

"*O*bserve now the cock," Lord Weyland said. "Who, in righteous victory, ruffles his feathers and struts with renewed vigor."

Cat smiled at Lord Weyland at her side. They were at the moment unobserved, having strolled out upon the terrace just above the rear garden. He did resemble a proud cock at that moment, she thought. Even in silhouette, she sensed the laughter in his eyes.

"A victory, is it then?" she asked.

"Absolutely. Handicapped by my sex as I am, the Fair Hen follows by my side. She marvels at me, and I at myself."

Cat laughed. "Lord Weyland, you must not be so vastly amusing. You distract me from my business."

"Ah. Yes, there is that." He paused by the balustrade, and she halted with him.

"Have you any further thoughts upon whom to choose as husband?" he asked.

Cat glanced back at the doorway. It seemed they were still alone. Lord Macclesby must have taken a moment to adjust his neckcloth.

"No, none whatever. Have you any observations?"

"Of course. Observing is what I do best. I observe, my dear Miss D'Eauville, that you are a martyr to your cause. You have my sincere admiration."

Cat decided not to rise to his bait. She gazed out over the darkness of the garden instead.

"It is so silent," she said. "There is nearly no sound at all here at night. You have no crickets."

"Is this a good thing, or a bad thing?"

She looked up at his shadowed face. "It is no sort of thing at all. If I wish to have crickets, I have only to set my future husband to the task of bringing them to me. After, of course, I have shot all of his partridges."

"Will this be before, or after, he travels to Africa?"

Cat smiled. Lord Weyland had been listening to her dinner conversation after all. "I *do* wish to go to Africa," she said.

He was silent for a long moment, gazing at her face. She was now uncertain of his mood. A moment before, she had been sure of it. Now she could not tell if his amusement had fled, or if he had merely adopted his usual style of English reserve.

"Does your father fully understand your wishes?"

She was so surprised by his question that she could not think of an answer. She was groping for it when a shadow darkened the doorway to the hall.

"Miss D'Eauville?"

It was Lady Ralston's voice. It contained a hint of anxiety, Cat noted. She sighed.

"I am here, cousin. Lord Weyland and I are having a very pleasant chat."

"There is a new arrival, my dear. Someone whom I know you will be very happy to meet."

Of all gentlemen, one he was sorry to see at Charles's home that evening. Lord Johnston.

Lord Weyland watched the tall young man with the easy smile foray into the room, straightaway making himself popular among the ladies. Johnston was a charming fellow; and that, unfortunately, was all Jack knew about him. It made him uneasy. For Miss D'Eauville was captivated, even from this distance, and he had not expected to see her so.

He did not like it. Yet, his duty was to Charles, and Charles needed him to be certain of Miss D'Eauville's attachment to an appropriate gentleman. Therefore he must learn what he could of Lord Johnston and, if need be, encourage the match.

If only the prospect did not gall him so!

"Who is the new gentleman?" Miss D'Eauville asked. She had not yet taken her eyes from Johnston since their reentrance into the ballroom. From the corner of Jack's eye, Jack saw Charles searching among the guests, a very intent expression on his ruddy face. Charles clearly wanted to effect an introduction between Miss D'Eauville and Johnston as soon as possible.

"He is Lord Johnston," Jack said. "I am afraid I do not know much about him."

"A pity." Miss D'Eauville glanced at Jack, but briefly, then fixed her gaze back on Johnston. Johnston had paused, and was speaking to a local matron and her pretty daughter. Jack almost sensed a competitive spirit emanating from Miss D'Eauville. Almost. It was not her nature to be jealous, for her self-confidence preempted the possibility.

"He is on my list, so therefore I know something of him," Miss D'Eauville said.

"That he is an earl wanting a rich wife, indubitably."

The rejoinder came in Charles's voice. "Yes, an earl!"

Jack turned to spot Charles emerging from the crowd. Charles paused between them, breathless, his smile conveying his satisfaction with the fortunate Lord Johnston.

"That is very good, indeed! What say you, Weyland?"

Before he could speak, Jack was trounced by the indomitable Miss D'Eauville.

"I am certain Lord Weyland will say something very interesting," she said, "but my introduction to Lord Johnston would be to better purpose."

"Of course," said Charles. "Delighted. Allow me."

Charles took Miss D'Eauville's arm and led her away—and that was the last time Jack spoke with her for the course of the entire long evening. For the first time since Jack could remember, the observation of human nature held no pleasure at all.

If this gentleman was not Cat's ideal, he was so very near it that it was difficult indeed to find cause to look further. He was possessed of perfect features and perfect teeth; he groomed and dressed himself well; and his smiling deference was all that she could ask for. Also, in addition to having already inherited an earldom, she understood his estate was very grand and very old, situated in Middlesex within a day's drive of London. Poor, charming, modest, handsome—what else could she desire? Only her father's blessing.

"Had I known such loveliness could exist in America, I should have long since sailed there and discovered you," Lord Johnston said. He pressed her gloved hand and smiled into her eyes.

They were in the refreshment room in a respite from dancing, and Cat took the opportunity to study her gallant more closely. The many-tiered candelabra from the table of delicacies glowed upon his face. The warm admiration she saw in his brown eyes appeared as sincere as she had imagined it to be in the light of fewer candles.

Cat suppressed the first sally that sprang to her lips— that had Lord Johnston known such a very rich shipbuilder's heiress resided in America, he would have made the voyage a *great deal* sooner—and shrugged, smiling at him. "With so many lovely ladies in England, I scarce think a gentleman would be tempted to search across an ocean."

"He is not. Hence I thank my lucky stars that I awaited the arrival of Miss Catherine D'Eauville."

"How can my arrival mean so very much to you, my lord?"

This time Cat watched the faintest flush of discomposure darken his complexion before he spoke.

"It should only mean much . . . if I were to entertain a certain aspiration, Miss D'Eauville. I have need to marry a lady of certain means. I had not hoped to feel so very much for her as well."

Cat gave her new admirer three points for honesty, and took away only one for flattery. Flattery, after all, was not difficult to hear. "My, my. And with such rapidity did your feelings arise!"

His color darkened a bit more. "So it must seem. I beg your pardon most humbly. I see I have done this ill. I am too much in haste . . . I *am* afraid of losing my chance with you. There, I have said it."

Cat gazed at his sorrowful expression and took pity on him. She had a sudden deep desire not to cause him pain; she wanted his good opinion, and did not want to see the hope fade from his very handsome dark eyes.

"You shall have your chance. But I warn you, I am not meek, and I have a great love of having my own way. I do not plan on changing."

"I should never wish it. How can I love a wild bird and wish for a tame canary?"

"In the same manner as any other man." Cat felt his fingers tighten on hers and withdrew her hand from his. She did not want to lose her head, after all. "Would you like to accompany me into the drawing room? I am in the mood to dance tonight. You may seek out other entertainment if you wish, of course."

He did not seek other entertainment. He returned with her to the drawing room, and to the disappointment of many of the gentlemen present, partnered her in the next set.

"I daresay, Jack, there has nothing untoward been discovered about the man. I see nothing the matter with my cousin choosing him."

"I simply say that insufficient has been discovered. Surely a little caution and time is a wise thing."

"My dear man, I am nothing if I am not cautious. Lord Johnston is said by every quarter to be a fine gentleman. That he has not left a trail of gossip for the wags is an excellent thing." Lord Ralston shifted uneasily in his seat. "I am not getting any richer, and if I must say so, my cousin is not getting any younger. How can you dispute the selection of Lord Johnston?"

Jack paced across his airy library, stopped at a tall window, and stared out between the open draperies. The morning sun gilded the row of limes at the distant border of his garden still, but the sparkle of dew was fading. Charles had arrived over a half hour prior to discuss Miss D'Eauville's marital prospects in privacy.

"I do not dispute. I suggest time be taken. Do not write to her father yet. I promise, you shall not die a poor man."

Charles sighed heavily from the upholstered armchair in which he was ensconced. "She does not have all the choices she imagines herself to have. You know this, I am sure of it. There are many who would consider my dear cousin too much the vulgar American to shackle themselves to her. All poor gentlemen have not lost their wits entirely."

"Hm. I did not realize that 'lack of wits' is a criteria on Miss D'Eauville's list."

"Of course it is! Somewhere on there it says, 'obeys mindlessly without the application of thumbscrews.' If that does not mean his garret is empty, I do not know what does."

Jack felt a smile tug at his lips in spite of himself. He turned round to regard his frustrated friend.

"No, and neither do I. But I can easily surmise another possibility . . . that the gentleman in question only presents himself as being so docile, while imagining himself with the power to alter Miss D'Eauville. And that, my friend, would be disaster indeed."

Charles's lower lip was protruding just slightly. Jack remembered a similar petulant expression on Charles from the days of their boyhood . . . as the time Jack had discovered that the trajectory of his new slingshot would serve to unseat Charles in a stream from some surprising distance.

"Be easy. I shall not let you down. We must simply be wiser than both your cousin and Lord Johnston. Let me think on this." Jack began to pace again, his mind fully engaged on the project. He reached the doorway and turned back, his gaze fixed unfocused on the Turkish rug beneath his feet. "If only we could place Miss D'Eauville and Lord Johnston together in circumstances where she acts quite herself . . . that could serve."

"I cannot think where she *does not* act herself."

"And acting herself would be . . . ?"

"Doing exactly as she pleases."

"Precisely. But as yet, so doing has not presented her suitors with any appreciable challenge."

"Damme, Jack, why should I want her challenging them?"

"Because ultimately, she will. And because the test should occur before the marriage, as opposed to after." Jack turned and faced Charles squarely.

"Should you want your cousin beaten by her husband?"

"Good gad, no!" Charles withdrew a kerchief from his coat and mopped his forehead. "Although, I do not believe there is a man who could do it. My cousin is a very healthy young woman—not to mention headstrong."

"Well, let us say, then, that we do not want to chance the possibility of such unfortunate marital strife."

"And how is this to be done?"

"Simply. By creating the strife before the marriage."

"That is the daftest thing I have ever heard!"

"I have faith that your cousin will know if such a tested gentleman would not suit. And the gentleman, if his garret is indeed occupied, will draw the sensible conclusion as well."

Charles groaned. "I am lost." Blotting his brow, he leaned back in the chair and closed his eyes. "Jack, you shall have to pay for my funeral. I shall die quite destitute after all."

"Of course not. Let me think upon this."

And think Jack did. After Charles departed, Jack remained alone in his library, lost in thought, occasionally withdrawing a volume from his shelves and placing it back, pacing to the window and gazing out, and pacing to the mantelpiece and fingering a classical figurine of Perseus holding the head of the Gorgon Medusa by her snaky hair. At last he went to his prized brass telescope and peered into the eyepiece, hoping for some distraction or inspiration.

He found it.

Lo and behold, here was his fair object, the Incalculable Miss D'Eauville herself, riding the verge of his property on one of Charles's good mares. She was making her morning escape, he knew. He wondered if she had encountered Charles. In any case, he saw no evidence of a following suitor this morning. Apparently, Lord Johnston was content to lie abed while his quarry rode about the countryside unescorted.

That was damned unfortunate. Nothing would infuriate Miss D'Eauville more than being followed.

She was an excellent vision on the mare, however. He could view her well enough to notice how easily and elegantly she sat her mount, riding with the kind of grace and strength he only observed in superior riders. He noted a slight smile on her lips, and smiled himself. He liked a woman who enjoyed the company of herself, a good horse and the countryside, and assuredly Miss D'Eauville did. She was no fainthearted damsel. She had said she wanted adventure, had she not? *I wish to travel. I wish to climb mountains. I wish to*

*ride upon an elephant. I wish to cross a gypsy's palm with
silver. Why should I be any different than you?*

Indeed.

He was yet observing the magnified vision of Miss
D'Eauville, and pondering where he might find an elephant, when Miss D'Eauville looked up. From her distance, she appeared to gaze straight at his window.
Then, before he could think to move, she took up the
spyglass at her neck.

Good gad, the woman rode equipped with a spyglass!
Jack straightened quickly, setting his precious telescope
wobbling on its stand. In a lightning movement he
saved it, both cursing his clumsiness and thrilling at the
contest. Quickly, he stepped back from the window.
Miss D'Eauville was indeed a woman to be reckoned
with! She was entirely too much like himself!

He kept his distance from the window, retreating
across the room to the mantelpiece for good measure.
Perseus and Medusa rested beneath his gaze.

"That's my good boy," Jack murmured to Perseus.
"Do not look at her, or all will be lost. A man must
keep all his wits about him in the presence of such a
fearsome female."

He heard a spray of small stones against his window
glazing. Freezing, he listened. It came again.

A faint feminine call came to him from outside.

Jack hesitated. Then he turned away from the mantelpiece and crossed to the window. Without hesitating, he
threw the casement open and leaned out. Medusa waited
below, eyeing him expectantly from the back of her horse.

"Good morning, Lord Weyland. I do believe you
have been spying on me." She gazed upward, awaiting
his answer.

"What a devilish thought. I should do nothing of
the kind."

"I saw the sun glance from your lens. It will not do
to pretend with me."

Jack met her unflappable gaze and realized that he had indeed been found out. "I was attempting to view a hawk."

"I did not see one."

"He flew away."

"Lord Weyland, shall you come out of your house, or must I tell your dear aunt about your very strange habits?"

Jack felt himself containing a laugh. "One moment, if you please." He closed the window. In a trice he had straightened his neckerchief, donned his coat, and descended the stairs, an urge to whistle barely suppressed. He expected to fully enjoy himself.

Miss D'Eauville awaited him on her mare. She was concluding another pass along the front of his house when he stepped out of his door.

"I see you have again outstripped your groom," he called cheerfully.

"Quite. Ah, but it does not do the least good to repine. However, do not attempt to divert me. I will now know about your telescope."

"Why, my charming Miss D'Eauville, there is little to know. I study the fauna with it." He smiled at her, and she smiled back at him.

"It must reward you with many happy hours of amusement."

"To be sure."

"It is not yet eight of the clock, and you have already breakfasted, received Lord Ralston, and spied upon the fauna. What a busy gentleman you are. I should not have disturbed you, but I was certain someone was looking upon me unawares from your window."

"I most humbly beg your pardon for causing you unease, Miss D'Eauville."

"I accept. But only if I may see this marvelous telescope of yours. I am certain your aunt would not mind my calling so early. We are quite intimate neighbors, after all."

She was setting up a challenge for him, Jack knew. And as his heart sped up, he wondered at her purpose. He doubted it was something to his advantage; it was most definitely something to hers. Whatever the case, she was surely doing just as she liked.

He also acknowledged his pleasure. Ah, he was a fool, looking upon his Medusa; even more the fool to let her into his intimate domain, where she was certain to divine his secrets. However, he must be brave if he were to divine her own. With luck he would devise a plan for her and Lord Johnston before she was on her way once more.

"My aunt would be happy to receive you," he said, "were she yet down. However, I do not mind extending the invitation myself. Would you please come in?"

Chapter Seven

*A*nother woman would have hesitated. However, as she was not another woman—what a lucky thing that was!—Cat did not flinch when Lord Weyland invited her into his dwelling. He dared her! Backing down was simply *not* to be thought of.

Cat gazed down at him from the back of her mare. "You must have your Thomas-the-Twin take my horse—if he is *indeed* your Thomas and not my cousin's Timothy."

Lord Weyland smiled up at her. "I shall call my 'Timothy-Thomas,' then. Helloa—he comes now. A clever lad."

In a trice the redheaded boy was leading her mare away, and Cat walked into Lord Weyland's spacious hall in his agreeable company. It looked bright and clean, as it had before—not a trace of dust on the inlaid rosewood occasional table they passed, and the polished marble tile gleamed in light from tall windows at the stair's first turning. It was to the stairs that Lord Weyland took her.

"Are you so certain you wish to view my lair?" he asked lightly as they mounted the steps.

"So long as it is not Hades, I cannot find an objection. I am certain it is a lair much like any other lair, with a telescope in it."

"My dear Miss D'Eauville, a gentleman's lair is *always* Hades."

"Then I shall take care to eat no pomegranates. I do not think I appear as foolish as that." They turned at the landing and continued on upward.

"Appearances can deceive," he said.

"Do I appear foolish or not foolish, Lord Weyland?"

"I shall not answer that question, for *I* am not foolish."

Cat laughed. "As you say—and yet, you trust me so completely. As a gentleman who would prefer not to marry, you should hope your pomegranates are all locked up, for I might seize them after all."

"My dear Miss D'Eauville, you may see my telescope, but pray have mercy upon me. I am but a poor scientific gentleman with an aunt to support."

"Poor" scientific gentleman or no, he claimed an impressive presence at her side. As they continued upward, Cat began to notice the warm place where his hand gently cupped her elbow. The warmth seemed to be spreading. An odd thing, that, for his hand did not vary in position or pressure; she took care to notice. And she was equally certain he carried himself no closer to her, and yet she felt him intimately in her space in a way she had not felt him a dozen steps before. She sensed his solidity, his stalwart bulk for all that his movement was smooth and graceful, his step quiet and light on the stair. She sensed his heat reaching across the space of air to touch with tentative fingers.

She *wanted* him closer to her, drat it all!

They reached the top of the stair.

"Follow me, my curious Miss D'Eauville. The mysteries of my telescope shall now unfold."

Cat walked with him to the open door to a chamber, her heart pounding mercilessly. She felt so *alive*. She could scarce think that to be caused by a telescope—indeed, she knew it to be the adventure, for this was one. She was about to peer into Lord Weyland's intimate domain and learn all of his precious secrets for herself.

They stepped inside. Cat was immediately struck by the size and warmth of the tower room, clearly a substantial library, with a large hearth to the rear and four tall casement windows to the front. A deep rose-and-black Turkish rug lay underfoot, and here and there about the room were scattered pieces of furniture and curiosities: armchairs, side tables, a set of brass scales, a bust of some historic gentleman or other on a pedestal, a massive terrestrial globe, and, of course, the telescope. It reposed on its delicate stand on a small table very near one of the windows.

Cat crossed to the window and gazed out. With the naked eye she could see some distance in the direction she had come. Stepping up to the telescope, she bent and peered through the eyepiece. At once, her gaze seemed to leap across the field.

"You must have very low-flying hawks," she said. "Your telescope is directed at the ground."

He hesitated for only a second. "I am afraid I jostled it. I do in general study the heavens. It is a most spectacular sight on a clear night."

Cat moved the telescope gently and panned the distant field. Lord Weyland had quite an interesting view—she could see most of the landmarks between here and her cousin Lord Ralston's estate.

She felt him move very close to her side. He made nearly no sound. She felt the tiny hairs prickle on the back of her neck.

It was no use. She straightened and turned to face him. "What other secret passions have you, Lord Weyland?"

He smiled. His gray-blue eyes twinkled; she liked the way his hair lay in disarray, as though he had plowed his fingers through it and forgotten. She began to notice the pulse in the base of her throat.

"Let me consider. I have a bag of very fine surgical instruments which I use to practice my animal medicine, and my horticultural experiments."

"I believe you spoke to me previously of your interest in studying humankind."

"Ah! You are quite right. How, then, may I and my secret passion serve you? Do you wish me to advise you again on your suitors?"

She gazed into his placid face. She felt a smile lurking in his eyes, and yet overall, his face was unreadable. As quickly as that, he had drawn the veil.

"You had nothing to say last night about Lord Johnston. Unfortunately, that is where I would have you be useful."

"Last night when you asked me for my thoughts, I had not yet observed our Lord Johnston, nor gleaned much of note about him. I have since had the chance to remedy that lack. And I have come to one absolute conclusion."

"And what is that?"

"That there is nothing whatever the matter with him."

Cat stared at Lord Weyland's face, trying to detect insincerity or jest of any kind. She saw none. Her adviser appeared to be absolutely serious.

Cat felt a knotting in her midsection that she was at a loss to understand. It was a feeling she was completely unaccustomed to.

"You seem distressed," he said softly.

Cat blinked. Lord Weyland's face focused above hers, with its smooth, pleasing lines, imperturbable lips, and observing eyes. The colors of the room merged behind them, blurring into the comfortable earth tones of the bookshelves.

Cat licked her lips. "I am not distressed. How could I possibly be distressed?"

Her voice fell echo-less in the carpeted room. Silence ensued. Cat gazed up into Lord Weyland's clear gray eyes and awaited his response. Instead, he only returned her gaze, much as if waiting for her to answer her own question. It felt, suddenly, as if her stomach were turning upside down and her heart had risen to somewhere between her ears, pounding so loudly her thoughts were scattered.

She decided to let Lord Weyland win the battle. "Let us do go down now—I detest being indoors forever." She turned from him, feeling like a coward and very disgusted with herself, but nonetheless convinced that Lord Weyland's particular Hades held great risk for her.

They descended the stairs, meeting no one and nothing but silence. The walk seemed much longer going down than it had in coming up, but Cat reserved speech until they stepped out-of-doors.

"Upon what facts do you form your opinion of Lord Johnston?" she asked.

His step was light in the grass beside hers as they slowly walked the length of the house toward his stable.

"Nothing untoward has been heard of him. Possibly disappointed in love once, if you are of a mind to be concerned. Apparently a certain young lady decided to wed a gentleman with deeper pockets."

"Is that all?"

"There does not seem to be anything to add. All that I have heard is singularly unobjectionable. Lord Johnston took his title at a tender age, with his uncle his trustee until he was twenty-one. His mother travels in elevated circles in London, but he does not seem to put in much more than an appearance there before returning to the country. This suggests the gentleman does not drink to excess, gamble, or entertain certain female friendships in town."

Cat studied the distance as she walked. "You feel, then, I should marry him."

"If that is what you feel yourself."

She looked at him. He turned his head and met her gaze, his eyes clear and benign.

"He is poor and of superior title, and from what one can learn, of good character as well. He appears to have easy manners, and is not likely to demand more of you than to produce his heir."

Cat found those words not at all reassuring. She frowned at Lord Weyland. "I rather think he is not in the position to demand anything at all."

Lord Weyland raised his expressive brows. "Miss D'Eauville, an heir is not a demand on the part of a gentleman of title. It is a need. And, I would suppose, it is your father's wish. Does he not want an earl for a grandson?"

Lord Weyland was right. She might wish him to the devil, but she could not dispute his words, no matter how much she wanted to. She had known, of course, that an heir came with the bargain . . . but somehow, she had not thought of that necessary duty coming upon her so quickly.

Cat pointed a gloved finger at him, waggling it for emphasis. "I shall not be rushed. I shall do what I please in my own time, and *then* I shall think about marriage and heirs."

"I see you perceive the difficulty," he said. "Time is resolute in its passing, I am afraid. It waits for none of us."

Time. In the space of their conversation, they had covered much of the distance between the house and the stable. With a constriction in her chest, Cat realized she was about to mount her mare and ride home to where her future husband awaited her.

It was too soon!

What was Lord Weyland saying . . . ?

". . . worth viewing. Perhaps you would like to go?"

She stopped, and he stopped as well. She stared at him. "What did you say?"

He blinked. "I was saying that there is an ancient ruin in reasonable travel distance, and I thought you might like to go. It is not to compare with traveling to Africa, of course."

"A ruin?"

"Yes. It is the remains of a bridge that crosses the Wye and a small fortification—quite crumbled, but interesting nonetheless. We could take a party of your guests and make a day of it." He paused. "And, if my information is accurate, there is a gypsy encampment in the vicinity. You did mention a wish to have your fortune told."

As she regarded him, she noticed that the twinkle was back in his eyes. A rush of delight surged through her.

"I definitely *should* like to go! What an excellent plan! Oh, yes! You shall come tonight and we shall make arrangements."

What an agreeable man Lord Weyland was! He had struck on just the right thing. Cat was in such an excellent mood that she barely noticed that Timothy-Twin seemed ready and waiting for her upon her return to Ralston. She cheerfully gave up her mare to him and rushed inside to form her plans.

The perfect plans were made. Lord Weyland visited that evening and explained the particulars of the site they were to visit, which by good fortune lay upon his own land. He had played there as a boy, as had Charles, Lord Ralston; and Cat could only presume that her father had, too. It made her even more excited to view the ancient structure.

Cat's unbridled pleasure was dampened the following day. A missive arrived from Weyland Hall stating that Lord Weyland and his aunt had received unexpected houseguests and would not be in the company. He urged all to attend without him with Lord Ralston as guide, but Cat realized that the day would be less pleasurable for her. After all, it was a site that Lord Weyland knew well, of which he must have many enlightening and entertaining things to say. Other gentlemen might be accommodating and amiable and make suitable husbands, but none of them would she enjoy as much—not even Lord Johnston, who continued to be entirely agreeable.

Lord Johnston fit all the criteria of Cat's list, and he fit them very well. She had yet uncovered no serious flaw. He was charming while appealingly modest; he was deferential and admiring and handsome. It was her good sense, she thought, that kept her searching for reasons to doubt. The fact that Lord Weyland had even *recommended* Lord Johnston, in fact, seemed to have the perverse effect of inducing her to search at greater length.

Cat continued to be determined on caution even on the following day, when Lord Johnston was so considerate as to absent himself with the other gentlemen to go shooting. Relieved at her solitude, Cat was on the point of going out when she found herself summoned.

"Come walk with me, Cat," Becky said.

Cat halted in the hall and faced her cousin, adjusting her gloves. "What is it, my dear? I was just about to go riding."

"Let us take a turn in the garden instead. I must speak with you."

Cat knew that her cousin never uttered such a thing without meaning it entirely, and knew she would not be dissuaded. But since making plans for the outing that was to take place a day hence, they had not spoken privately, and Cat found she longed for Becky's sensible speech.

"Very well. Let us see what blooms today."

They exited by the front door and started around the manor through the manicured lawn. Cat caught the fragrance of sweet rose in new bloom, and saw that Becky was pensive, even for her.

"You seem set upon Lord Johnston," Becky said.

"I should not say I am precisely set upon him, but he is a delightful gentleman. He does seem to suit, does he not?"

"You shall not choose Lord Rhodes, that is quite certain?"

Cat raised her brows inquiringly as she gazed at her cousin, but the expression was wasted as Becky stared straight ahead, a small frown puckering her forehead.

"As to that, I do not think it likely. Lord Johnston is more to my taste."

"Then you should make your feelings known, Cat. Lord Rhodes still hopes you may agree to have him. He would not stay, else."

"My, how you guard poor Lord Rhodes! He could not have a better champion than you."

"Do not joke. He is a serious man, a bit melancholy perhaps, but he is a loving father, and as sincere a gentleman as I have met. He needs your decision."

"You offer no opinion?"

"I know it would be useless for me to do so. I will say that he comes on your outing tomorrow in hopes of speaking with you, and I think you will spend the whole of your day with Lord Johnston. It is unkind to allow that to happen."

"It is not as though one cannot find pleasure in the trip. It is quite a large party, and I am not the only source of entertainment. Lord Rhodes will have plenty of distractions—as will I." But not, Cat thought to herself, nearly as much distraction as she would have had with Lord Weyland present. How annoying the disappointment was. But perhaps it was just as well—she needed her attention for her hopeful beaux.

"I rather think Lord Rhodes would prefer to return to his home and his children, if there is nothing more substantial for him to gain by staying."

"Good heavens, has it occurred to you that he may meet with precisely what he is looking for tomorrow?

There are to be other single young ladies in the party, and one may suit. You are not being sensible, Becky. That is not like you."

"I do not know whom he might choose. He has met them all except for Lord Weyland's fiancée, and he will not be stealing *her* away."

"Fiancée?" Cat stopped, and Becky stopped beside her. Cat stared at her cousin. "I had not known Lord Weyland to be engaged!"

Becky blinked. "As to that, I only know that Lady Ralston referred to 'his young lady' visiting him, as their guests are the Millingtons. I believe Susan understands from Miss Southrop that there are expectations of a match from that quarter."

Cat felt a swell of urgency and annoyance. She did not know which emotion was greater; she only knew that a clenching agitation had risen up within her, illogical but real.

"He does not want to marry. He said so himself. I cannot believe it."

Becky's solemn gaze held her own. "I do not know his wishes. I only know what I have heard. He may feel it is advisable to do other than he wants."

"Oh, bother the man!" Cat started up again, taking long, angry strides, forcing Becky to hurry to keep up. "I thought he would not do something he did not wish to do! He has no desire to marry! He has said so! He said that he would rather dance—Oh, never mind!"

"I do not know what difference it makes," said Becky from behind. "You will not marry Lord Weyland, so why may he not marry someone else? It will do you no good at all if he does not."

"You can not know," snapped Cat, "what may do me good and what may not do me good. If anyone in the world knows, it is myself."

"And what would do you good, then?"

"I cannot possibly form an opinion when I am not allowed a moment to think!" Cat steamed on a moment longer, until her thoughts were called to the sound of Becky puffing behind her in a valiant attempt to keep up. Cat stopped and turned toward her cousin. Becky was flushed, her forehead damp with perspiration. Cat felt instant guilt.

"Do not mind me, Becky. Although I suppose it is no wonder if you do! I am being a horrid crosspatch."

"Yes, you are," Becky said, coming to stand beside her. "But more important is *why* you are being a crosspatch. I do believe it has to do with your feelings for Lord Weyland, but, of course, I would never presume such a thing. I am sure you have your own thoughts on the matter."

"Of course I do! And I do not have any such feelings for Lord Weyland. How absurd. I should have to be foolish and hen-witted besides!"

"That is true," Becky said. "And, of course, you are neither of those."

"Certainly not. I have no 'feelings' for any gentleman who is not on The List. I should never allow myself to have them."

"Is it not a fortunate thing," Becky said then, "that you are so very sensible."

"I am incapable of being otherwise," said Cat.

Her opinion of herself continued until they entered the morning room to discover Lady Ralston all smiles, seated before her tea tray and holding a piece of folded correspondence in her hand.

"There you are!" she exclaimed happily. "My dears, I have the most excellent news. I have a note from Lord Weyland this morning, saying that he and his aunt will accompany us on the excursion after all. But it is even more agreeable than that. Their houseguests shall come also. Is that not a happy addition?"

Chapter Eight

*H*er name was Augusta Millington, and her father was Mr. Thomas Millington, the wealthy owner of an ironworks. Mrs. Millington was the daughter of a viscount, and a sometime friend of Miss Southrop's.

The Millingtons rode in their own carriage from Weyland, so Cat could not closely examine Lord Weyland's young lady until their arrival at Oldford on Wye. Her thoughts were much occupied with the little glimpse she had had of Miss Millington being handed into her father's coach at Weyland, where they had all assembled their conveyances prior to setting out. The rest of her attention was distracted by the conversation in the carriage between Lady Ralston, Becky, Miss Carter, and herself.

"Yellow sprigged muslin," declared Lady Ralston's young friend Miss Carter, withdrawing her gaze from her window, "and the most darling straw bonnet, and ribbon to match!"

"She must have a respectable marriage portion," said Lady Ralston. "I do believe they are driving a newish carriage. What do you think, Miss D'Eauville?"

Cat, at the moment, was annoyed at how the plumes from her high-crowned hat were rubbing the roof, which she blamed for her present mood.

"She seems very pale, and no bigger than a minute."

"I believe she is very young," said Becky.

"I think Lord Weyland is the *most* agreeable man! I am sorry he is taken!" Miss Carter beamed at her traveling companions. "She is so very pretty. I am sure that must be why he fell in love with her."

Cat pulled at her hat. "Nonsense. Appearance has very little to do with it. Neither does love."

The carriage set forth with a jerk. Cat made a sound of vexation and seized her hat with both hands.

"It is a very peculiar thing, then," Becky said. "I should have thought *one* of those things counted for part of it."

"She may have a list of her own upon which Lord Weyland's name appears." Lady Ralston smiled mischievously. "Like yours, Miss D'Eauville."

"What list are you speaking of?" queried Miss Carter.

Cat pulled the offending hat off her head, causing Becky to duck the lash of burgundy ostrich plumes.

"Marriage is a business to enter into with much forethought," Cat said. "I should not have made an announcement of it, but since Lady Ralston has, I shall explain it. I have a very precise list of eligible gentlemen that represents months of careful consideration."

"Really!" Miss Carter's eyes grew round.

"I assisted, as this was scarcely a thing Miss D'Eauville could do from America," Lady Ralston said. "And I do believe we have made a success of our project!"

"It is not a done thing yet."

"But my dear Miss D'Eauville, surely Lord Johnston is just the gentleman we have been seeking. Do you not agree? Lord Ralston and I were just speaking of it last night. He is an earl, is very nice in his manners, and is handsome as well!"

Cat felt the steady pressure of Becky's gaze, and knew the instant Becky released her and looked out the window. Becky's words of the previous day, however, repeated themselves in Cat's head. Becky was wrong! Cat did *not* have feelings for Lord Weyland. Lord Johnston, on the other hand, was delightfully compliant. He was just the sort of gentleman she needed.

"I agree, Lady Ralston. I believe Lord Johnston will do very well."

No matter how determinedly Cat set her mind on Lord Johnston, she found that her heart was not settled. This was proved at the moment Lord Weyland's carriage drew up to their picnicking spot, slipping alongside those already arrived, and her spirits flew upward like a cork coming free of a sunken flask.

Lord Weyland rode alongside the carriage, looking quite handsome in his riding coat and beaver hat, his upright, easy posture on the horse a thing Cat fully appreciated. Had she noticed before how well he sat his horse? And how she wished she had the mare. A fleet image of Lord Weyland and herself riding across the meadow, laughing and trading verbal parries, intruded.

Lord Weyland drew up his horse beside the now stopped carriage, made a gesture of welcome to the gathering, and began to dismount. Cat started forward.

A hand fell upon her arm. "Cousin—"

Cat turned and leveled her gaze at cousin Charles's flushed face.

"What is it, dear?"

The answer was immediately apparent, for Lord Johnston stopped at Charles's side. Lord Johnston smiled. "At last! I thought the journey would never end."

Cat gazed up into his kindling eyes. "Really? I should have thought it more pleasurable for you, upon a horse rather than within an ill-sprung carriage."

"I should have preferred the carriage."

"Ah, then you should have spoken, and I should have taken your horse."

"I meant, my Miss D'Eauville, that I should have preferred to be at your side." Lord Johnston's smile continued. "You possess such a delightful sense of whimsy."

"I am *very* glad you like it," said Cat. The breeze flipped one of her burgundy plumes down and tickled her forehead. She brushed it away, taking the moment to glance back toward Lord Weyland.

Darn! He was handing Miss Millington down from their carriage. She saw Miss Millington alight, then watched Miss Millington smile shyly up at Lord Weyland as he yet held her small hand in his. And Lord Weyland . . . it looked perhaps as if he might be enjoying himself. Was there a smile in his eyes? Cat could not see from here. He was so very much taller than the diminutive Miss Millington that his head was bent down and slightly away from Cat, as if listening to catch the sound of Miss Millington's very breathing. Yes . . . no . . . yes. Would the girl not speak more loudly? Would Lord Weyland not turn this way, even a small bit?

"Miss D'Eauville?"

Cat turned back to Lord Johnston. He still wore a smile, but it seemed a trifle strained.

"Do you not like to eat in the open air?" he asked. "I believe it is the most delightful thing."

"Of course she does," Charles said, his tone jovial. "My cousin is quite the one for picnics. She has had much experience picnicking. Is that not so, Miss D'Eauville?"

Cat gave one last wistful glance toward Lord Weyland and Miss Millington. It appeared that Miss Millington's parents and Lord Weyland's aunt were all of the group now, in amicable conversation. All seemed to be smiling, except Mr. Millington, who appeared to be bored.

Cat sighed and looked back at Lord Johnston. "In America we are forever picnicking," she said. "We are famous for it. Indeed, it is an oddity for us to live within doors."

"Miss D'Eauville," Charles murmured tightly.

Lord Johnston blinked. "You are so very amusing, Miss D'Eauville."

"I simply crave amusement, you see, and when it is lacking I must provide my own. Here we are, all arrived, and we stand about chatting! We have all of this lovely meadow to explore, and the copse ahead, and whatever thing waits around the bend in the stream." Cat cast her glance around her, and spied Lady Ralston directing the servants, her friend Miss Carter close at hand; she saw two other loose knots of guests in conversation; and another, standing somewhat aside, that consisted of Becky and Lord Rhodes alone.

Charles cleared his throat. "It is an ordinary thing to chat while in company," he said, a trace of irritation in his voice. "The servants are setting up the tables and chairs, and we have naught to do but stand!"

"If I may speak, I shall take Miss D'Eauville's part. We may walk as easily as not."

Cat cast an appreciative look at Lord Johnston and smiled. "You have the heart of a true gentleman," she said. "Come then, and walk with me."

Cat extended her elbow, and Lord Johnston willingly took it. "With pleasure."

No one followed, so Cat realized that her cousin Charles was affording Lord Johnston and herself some moments of privacy. Indeed, there was no pain in walking at the side of a very handsome, agreeable man, and it afforded her the chance to know him better—a thing she had best pursue.

"How lovely it is to walk with you on this perfectly charming day," Lord Johnston said.

"And what a pretty picture this landscape is. See how the meadow slopes upward toward that line of trees."

"That, I believe, is the bank of the river."

"Yes, of course it is. We must walk closer to see the water." Still walking at Lord Johnston's side, Cat looked behind her. She could glean no more of value of Lord

Weyland and Miss Millington, save she could identify
Weyland by his height and Miss Millington by her miss-
ish yellow gown.

"I love the sound of your voice. It is like bells on
the wind."

Cat tore her gaze away from the teasing sight behind
them and glanced up at Lord Johnston. He gazed down
at her, his eyes partially hooded and his lips sensuously
slack. He did not look like a man who was paying the
least attention to where he was walking.

"I must take a care, then, that the wind does not
catch my tongue."

"Miss D'Eauville—how amusing you are!"

"I wonder if the old bridge is very near? I hope we
catch view of it soon."

"I should as soon never see the bridge. I am all full
of the sight of you."

Cat was worldly enough to know that the man was
speaking love to her. Her trouble was that she had not
the desire to receive it—an unfortunate thing, but there
it was. An unromantic streak had always been a distinct
trait of hers.

Almost always.

*Good Lord, Cat, he is as handsome a man as you will find.
But you will be so particular.*

"Do not talk such silliness. You may see me anytime.
The bridge is a rare antiquity."

"In my eyes, you are a thing much more rare."

They were near the water's edge now, an outcropping of trees and bush obscuring what lay around
the bend. She did so want to see it—if only Lord Johnston would keep his enthusiasm for her in check for
a little longer.

"You are kind. Presently, this 'Rarity' does very much
want to see the ruin. Be good and indulge me, or I shall
have to send you away."

"I-I humbly beg your pardon! I shall be all compliance. Not a contrary word shall I speak. I shall do nothing but give you my utmost assistance."

"Apology accepted."

Cat stepped in front of him and began to climb the grassy grade to the trees, stepping around small outcroppings of stones. The shade of the first bough fell over her, and she could hear the rapids of the Wye below. She also heard Lord Johnston's anxious steps behind her.

She pressed on. Skirting the trunks of several tall trees and wild shrubs, she stepped out at last onto a grassy ledge. There was the Wye—some twenty yards across and as many feet below them.

He came up beside her and stood still. Yet, Cat felt alone. It was an inexplicable thing, but he felt as if he were far away.

Cat stood in silence, staring over the water. Here it widened to a small river, with a swift current, and deep enough to carry small boats. On the opposite shore, Cat saw at the water's edge a parade of trees that climbed a considerable bank to what appeared to be the roadway above.

What would she miss if she married Lord Johnston? Would she always wonder? Cat felt restless at the direction her thoughts were taking. She did, absolutely, need to make her father happy; his entire life's goal had been for his child to marry well. After that marriage, which she meant to accomplish with as little inconvenience to herself as possible, she had believed that her life was her own for the living. But would she have regrets?

A flash of color and movement caught her eye. She could tell for certain there was a roadway across the river now, as there was a procession of donkey-drawn carts and a mixed group of persons traveling alongside on foot. Many of the women wore bright skirts and shawls, and she could hear the faint clinking and creaking of the moving wagons. A child's cry carried across on the breeze, and then a burst of male laughter.

"The gypsies!" Cat said softly. She watched the slow caravan with consuming interest. "Where can they be going?"

"To the next town, to be sure," Lord Johnston said. "I imagine they have worn out their welcome in Oldford."

"Oldford? But that was where we were going to see the fortune-teller. We were to have traveled there after luncheon. They must have just removed from there. Oh, drat!"

"Well, there is a disappointment," said Lord Johnston, "but I admit I feel relief. I am rather uneasy about them."

"Uneasy? Why should one be uneasy? They are businesspeople, after all, and we are only proposing to give them some." Cat picked up her skirts and began walking determinedly along the edge of the rise above the river.

"My dear Miss D'Eauville, where are you going?"

"The bridge is this way, is it not? I must hurry, or they will be gone. You need not come."

"What! You cannot be thinking of crossing that old relic! It is quite out of use, and dangerous besides!"

"I can at least examine it."

Cat heard the faint sounds of Lord Johnston striding behind her.

"Wait. You cannot! It is risky, and—and simply not done. Miss D'Eauville, you know very well that you *cannot* cross that bridge."

"Of course, I can. You may tell the others that I shall not be long."

Cat could not put words to the urgency that came over her to see the gypsies and have her fortune read. She breathed deeply and exuberantly. Her senses deepened. Her legs felt like running, as much as they were encumbered by her skirt. Her booted feet, however, made sure steps through the grass and over small stones. Freedom! Adventure! They called to her, pulling her away from all the obligations, the expectations, and the Lord Johnstons of the world.

The land came to a gentle point guarded by a large old oak. Cat stepped around the tree and saw her goal. Before her stretched a narrow span of stone, supported by two large pylons of ancient rock. In the center of the span, however, a large chunk of stone had sometime since fallen away.

Cat scampered up the grassy rise at the foot of the bridge and stepped upon the worn, sunken stone of the ancient road. Facing the bridge, she gave it brief study.

The relic crossed the river at some height, given the elevation of the riverbanks that it connected. The flat span was no more than a dogcart wide, with no wall along its length, requiring care be taken in crossing it— particularly the broken section in the middle, of which only a very narrow portion remained.

In that place, Cat determined, it was the width of a man only. But this was wide enough.

"Miss D'Eauville! You must stop this instant!"

Lord Johnston's command was in vain. Cat stepped out upon the bridge.

Chapter Nine

"*M*iss D'Eauville, you must come back. It is very dangerous!"

Cat's next step, should she wish to proceed, would be upon the narrow span of rock that remained intact in the center of the bridge. The breadth of the span was possibly sixteen inches, and its length was some five feet until the bridge became its normal width again. It was a daunting task to continue, especially when she stood some twelve feet above the swift current, listening to it rush around the rock support. Additionally, there was the distraction of Lord Johnston standing at the foot of the bridge behind her, highly agitated and seeming not to know what to do with himself.

"I shall come after you!" he cried.

"No, you will not," Cat said. "I do not believe this bridge can hold the two of us." Cat took a deep breath, released it, took careful hold of her skirts and set forth. Whatever Lord Johnston uttered next, she did not hear. She was completely focused on the narrow slab of stone below her feet.

One step—good. Second step—good. Third step—she extended her arms. For an alarming moment she wavered, then recovered her balance. *Carefully, now.* Four, five, six—victory! Cat glanced back with a grin of satisfaction. Her heart pounded, and she was tempted to dance about on the center of the old bridge. However, reason prevailed. There was nothing to say that another piece of rock could not dislodge, and more importantly, the gypsies were escaping her.

She waved cheerfully at the distraught Lord Johnston, who had progressed but a few steps from the foot of the bridge. "You see! I have succeeded! Do not wait for me—I shall be back presently!" She turned and scampered the rest of the way to the opposite side.

The gypsies were yet within sight. There was no time to lose. She hiked up her skirts again, doubled her pace, and called out.

"Helloa! Wait, please!"

In the most brief of moments she caught the attention of a group of small children straggling at the rear of the column. Some hesitated, but others dashed toward her. Cat soon found herself surrounded with ragged, barefoot, dark-skinned, bright-eyed children, their elfin faces alive with curiosity and wonder. They were all of them small, but Cat guessed the eldest were older than they appeared. In their dark eyes she saw knowing that was beyond the age their stature suggested.

"How lovely you all are!" Cat bent low and brushed back a long black strand from the eyes of the small girl. An older girl quickly caught the child's arm and pulled her away.

A thin boy pressed in front of them. "Please," he said. "Please give." He held out a dirty hand. Simultaneously, as though on cue, all of the children did the same. "Please! Please! Missus, please!"

"Oh, heavens. Have I not a sweet?" Cat muttered. She searched her waist purse, and besides the usual contents, several spare pins and an embroidered silk handkerchief, she discovered two peppermints twisted in paper. This was hardly sufficient for such a large group.

A sharp barked command brought her head up. The children melted back. Before her stood three young men, dark and sinewy and lean and dressed in the plain stuff of gypsy men. One wore a large gold earring; all carried knives at their waists.

"What do you want?" said one. His dark eyes penetrated, and gave Cat the feeling he saw more than he ought.

She drew herself up straight. She was easily of his height, and taller than his companions, and she thanked her father again for her stature. "Good day, gentlemen. I am Miss D'Eauville, I am visiting from America, and I should like my fortune told." She smiled broadly. The sun felt pleasant on her face, the sky was cloudless, and her blood rushed warmly.

The man glared at her. "What have you to give?" His look touched upon the gold brooch at her throat.

Cat raised her chin and held his stare. "I shall pay a fair price, of course. No more, no less. Is your fortune-teller available today? I meant to find you in town, but I see you are traveling elsewhere."

His black eyes grew hard. Cat gazed back, unflinching. Then he blinked.

"I will see if she will meet with you. Come with us."

"Very well."

She noted, of course, that her accompanying them might not be strictly a matter of her choice; the other two gentlemen fell in behind her, and she sensed that the gypsy caravan was her only possible destination. However, since this was what she wanted, she decided it was not yet time to be concerned.

They reached the waiting caravan in a moment. Everyone—the other men, the women, and the remaining children—were gathered outside the wagons staring at her, asking questions and making comments in a language she could not understand. They were clearly trying to determine what to make of her. They were also, she knew, guessing at the contents of her purse.

She stopped and stood still, gazing at the curious group and keeping an eye on the covered wagon the English-speaking gypsy had disappeared within. This wagon was older than some, and its paint, although faded and peeling, was more elegant than the plain decoration of the other wagons. The curtains at the rear of it were of a fringed brocade, very faded and plagued with holes, but proclaiming status within the group.

The waiting became somewhat awkward. "Well," she said at last, "have you been in this country long? I have not. It is lovely, do you not agree?"

This elicited a barrage of exclamations within the group, and several of the women laughed.

"Ah, but you have not bears here. I understand the worst you have are wild hogs. Of course, wild hogs are enough trouble in themselves. But they would make better stew."

At all appearances, she was succeeding in amusing the group, no matter that they did not understand a word she said. Still, the gypsy gentleman did not come back out of the wagon, and everyone continued to stand and stare at her. It was plain that there was not much to sustain them but the land, the donkeys that drew their wagons, and one rough-coated brown horse. It seemed to Cat that they meant to have her to dinner, but could not decide whether as a guest or as the main course.

Cat smiled at the gypsies, held her purse tightly, and wondered if Lord Johnston would come to her rescue should it be necessary. She hadn't considered the qualities of courage or heroism on her list, but surely any gentleman would see the wisdom of saving the heiress he meant to marry.

Of course, she would never need a rescue. It would be too humiliating and so disappointing. Men had the oddest quality of believing themselves superior after such an event, as well, something she would never tolerate in a husband.

Perhaps some other gentleman might come after her. Heavens—if one of them succeeded, she might be expected to marry him instead! If Lord Macclesby were to come, it would be too ridiculous. Then she thought of Lord Weyland.

He, of course, was encumbered with Miss Millington. It was entirely too bad, for he seemed the least likely to kick up a fuss about her adventure.

"My lady, she will see you."

Cat turned in surprise, and found the young gypsy man on the back step of the fortune-teller's wagon, watching her intently. It was on the tip of her tongue to correct his address of her, but she thought better of it.

"Very good!"

He held the curtain back. She drew in a breath and mounted the narrow plank steps. Then she peered inside.

She was met by darkness and the dizzying perfume of incense. What else might be within, for good or for ill, she could not tell.

Here, truly, was her adventure.

"Lord D'Eauville! I need you!"

Jack turned from his idle conversation with Mr. Millington and Charles at the sound of Lord Johnston's voice. The sight of Lord Johnston dashing toward them, oblivious of decorum and fashion, stopped the words in his throat.

"She is crossing the old bridge! She is—"

Lord Johnston came to a stop, gasping for breath.

"Gad, save me," groaned Charles. "It is Miss D'Eauville!"

"Charles, let him speak."

Lord Johnston gulped in another breath. "Miss D'Eauville. She spied the gypsies on the other side. I could not stop her."

"I knew it!" cried Charles. "She is running off with gypsies! I am ruined!"

Jack placed his hand on Lord Johnston's shoulder. "Johnston, do you mean to say she is crossing the bridge to see the gypsies?"

"Yes. To have her fortune told. And the gypsies have got her!"

"Miss D'Eauville has been taken by gypsies?"

Jack turned to yet another astounded face. Mr. Millington looked both shocked and perplexed.

"Apparently so. I suggest we follow her."

Jack turned with the intention of seeking his horse, only to face Miss Millington's aghast countenance. She was, Jack saw, staring at Lord Johnston in his stricken state.

"Oh, sir, are you quite all right?" she cried.

Jack wheeled about and sought his horse. Flagging his groom, they set about the task together. In moments his mount was saddled, and Jack turned his horse toward the Wye.

Charles and Lord Johnston were already out of sight around the bend by the river.

Chapter Ten

*T*he curtain fell closed behind her. For a moment Cat stood in inky darkness; then she made out the shape of a low, quilt-covered cot at the side of the wagon. A small leather-bound trunk next to the cot supported a candle on a tin plate, as well as several smoky wands of burning incense.

The thin form beneath the quilt spoke. "Sit."

The gypsy's bright dark eyes stared out of a thin wrinkled face that danced in the shadows of the candle flame. There was a stool at the foot of the cot, and Cat sat down.

"You are from America," the gypsy said in a surprisingly strong voice.

"I did say as much. Now, shall you tell my fortune? I am quite ready for it."

The lacework of wrinkles on the old woman's face moved into a slight smile. "You are impatient."

"Yes, but that is something that I know."

"And I am to tell you what you do not know. Sit quietly for a moment."

"Do you not need a crystal ball, or tea leaves, or some such? Will you only lie there and speak?"

"I do not need those things. I am old enough to see without them. Now, silence."

Cat sat and listened to the sound of the old woman

breathing. There was a faint wheeze, a catch, and then the gypsy coughed. More silence followed—too much silence. Cat began to worry. Peering at the old woman in the dim candlelight, she detected that she was yet breathing.

"I see a rich, handsome man," the gypsy said.

"Oh, that cannot be right. I cannot marry a rich man."

"Hush! The picture is fading!"

"I am sorry."

The old woman took a slow, rasping breath.

"I also see a poor man. You will choose one."

"Is there only one poor man?"

The gypsy huffed. "Shall I continue, or shall you tell your own fortune?"

"Please go on."

"You will know which rich man and which poor man. You will marry one of them. But you must be certain to choose wisely. Things are not as they seem. Happiness will not come in the way you think it will."

Cat acknowledged some disappointment. The fortune-teller did not seem able to tell her much, after all. And truth to tell, the woman seemed quite ill. Possibly, this affected her ability to tell the future.

"He will cross water for you."

"Who will cross water?"

"The man you will marry."

"That is impossible. I am the one who crossed water, to come to England. I must marry an English lord."

"Will you stop speaking? I tell you what I see! I cannot help what it is!"

"I beg your pardon."

"He will cross water. Remember my words. Of this I am certain."

Cat heard gentle breathing. It seemed the old woman's eyes were closed now. She had said all she had to say.

"Thank you," Cat said softly. She stood. Then she

silently removed her gold broach. Leaning over the cot, she picked up the woman's gnarled hand and placed the broach in her palm.

"For the children," Cat said, and she began gently folding the fortune-teller's knobby fingers over the brooch.

The old woman's eyes fluttered open. For a moment she held Cat in her powerful stare. Then her expression relaxed. Her fingers curled around the brooch.

"You will do the right thing," the gypsy said. "Now go, and meet your gentleman."

When Miss D'Eauville appeared in the curtained doorway of the gypsy wagon, Jack decided that she seemed a queen appearing to her people. The children crowded about the foot of the wagon laughed and waved; Miss D'Eauville laughed and waved back; and the young man Istvan stood by to assist her down the steps. She descended, of course, with no help at all.

Jack stood by his mount's head and patted the uneasy horse on the nose. All was well. He was wet to his knees and lighter by the coins he had given to Istvan, but Miss D'Eauville was none the worse for her adventure, and he had no need for the pistol beneath his coat.

At that moment Miss D'Eauville spotted him. He saw the flash of surprise cross her face, to be quickly replaced by an expression of delight.

"Lord Weyland! How good to see you here! Did you wish your fortune told? I am afraid she is tired, the old dear."

He stifled a smile. "Then I came all this way, and wet my boots, all for a severe disappointment?"

She came up to him, her face alight. "I am afraid so. And now you must journey back again. Tell me, did you fall from the bridge?" Her gaze went to his mount. "A horse could never pass over it."

"That is very astute of you." Jack waved to the gypsy Istvan, and then gestured to Miss D'Eauville to approach his horse. "Lord Johnston fell from the bridge. Charles was afraid to cross it, as he always has been, and stayed to help Lord Johnston from the water. Lord Rhodes, I believe, went to seek a boat." He cupped his hands to receive her neatly booted foot. "I chose to ford the river with my trusted mount."

She laughed and placed her foot in his hands, and he lightly tossed her up. In a moment he was mounted behind her, and directed his horse toward the river.

"How very lucky that you knew a place to ford. I am perfectly capable of recrossing the bridge, however."

"As I am reluctant to leave my horse behind, perhaps you could indulge me with your company."

She laughed again. Her shoulder and hip were warm against him, and he felt his heart squeeze. Ah, the incomparable Miss D'Eauville! Impossible and delightful and untouchable. As much as he wanted to put his arms around her, he wanted even more for the temptation to pass. It was just so unfortunate that Aunt Bea had invited the Millingtons . . . not that he was enthused about the match with Miss Millington, but Aunt Bea did fuss so about his single state, and since he could not have Miss D'Eauville . . . well, he guessed there would be the devil to pay with the Millingtons now.

He found he did not care. But he found he *did* care, very much, about the feeling inspired by the delightfully soft Miss D'Eauville tucked so close to his body— so much so that he prayed that Miss D'Eauville did not discover how much! It was a nuisance he had not anticipated. He was no schoolboy, but a man of science!

"I do not know," she said, "but I have the oddest suspicion that you all meant to rescue me. I know how very strange that seems, but yet I do not think my fortune, or yours, is of that much moment to you."

"Come to your rescue? Oh, not I. I should never admit to something so ill-advised."

"I thought as much."

"I might tell you that the gypsies could have stolen

all you had, but never would I presume you needed rescuing."

"I should hope not. Besides, I should simply give them everything. There was nothing I carried I could not spare."

"It is a matter of perspective, I suspect, although you should keep in mind that a lady's clothing can bring a very good price. I rather think you would not have liked returning to us in the raiment you were born in."

"Oh," she said. "No, that might have been a trifle too exciting. I should not have allowed that."

"I see." He fought to keep the laugh from his voice. His self-control nearly failed. At the moment they were beginning the steep descent to the river, and he was abruptly pressed quite firmly against Miss D'Eauville's very delectable hip.

"So, will you marry Miss Millington?" Cat asked.

It was fortunate that he was using his remaining concentration in guiding his horse down the bank. It served to excuse his silence as he grappled for a response. Miss D'Eauville swayed between his arms, vulnerable in her side-mounted position, but did not seem at all anxious. Conversely, he felt the waves of excitement coming from her that told of her liking for the adventurous ride . . . or perhaps, from more than that.

"Have you made that deduction, then? It is a possibility. Although, I do not know what her thoughts will be after I so presumptuously left her to seek my fortune among the gypsies."

Miss D'Eauville was silent for a moment. They reached the water's edge, and his gelding waded in.

"I am sorry," she said quietly. "I did not mean for anyone to come after me."

"But you are not surprised that they did."

"No. Not in afterthought. I did not think about it at all when I first crossed the bridge."

"That is what I thought. You would make an excellent

military mind, my dear. Nothing distracts you from your purpose."

"Do not make me seem ridiculous, Lord Weyland. For I shall make you seem more so, you can be certain."

The gelding was above his knees in water now, choosing his steps carefully. Miss D'Eauville reached down and grasped a handful of her skirt, gathered it safely above the rising water, and pressed against Jack as she did so. Her action was completely unself-conscious and wholly practical.

Jack smiled grimly to himself. When one carried a woman on one's horse with her ankles on display and her most enticing form pressed against one, one dreamed of circumstances considerably different than those Miss D'Eauville presented. As it was, his fancy was rapidly outstripping his sense.

Clinging to logic as a dog clings to a bone, he spoke. "I admit to puzzlement. I cannot see how you can make me seem more ridiculous than I do now. My boots are soaked, my kerchief is askew, and Lord Johnston will likely shoot me in a jealous rage."

"I should not think it ridiculous to be shot."

"There is comfort, at least."

"And as for Lord Johnston, I will not let him shoot you. I shall refuse to marry him if he does."

"Pray, then, tell him your intentions before he shoots, else we will both be done in."

The horse was up to his belly now. As the water rushed around them, he fell silent, minding the horse's faltering step in the deep water. For an alarming moment, the horse slipped and staggered. Miss D'Eauville swayed, and Jack instinctively put a steadying arm around her. She slid back against him again, firmly against his thigh. Jack clenched his teeth.

The horse regained his footing. Miss D'Eauville turned her head and gazed up at him. There was some-thing surprised and wondering in her eyes. Her face was a delicate pink.

Jack sucked in a breath, and realizing he still held her, took his arm away. Miss D'Eauville abruptly looked forward.

It was the longest godforsaken ride in his life. Even such a ride had an end, however. As they approached the river's edge, figures appeared on the bank above. Miss D'Eauville looked up at them and waved.

"I have had my fortune told!" she called. "Guess what the gypsy said to me!"

Miss D'Eauville's quiet cousin Miss Prescott returned a halfhearted wave from above. "I hope," Miss Prescott said dryly, "that she foresaw you living until your wedding day."

"I still say you have much to answer for," scolded Becky. "The Millingtons are humiliated, Lord Weyland is humiliated, cousin Charles and dear Susan are humiliated, Lord Johnston is humiliated—"

"Are you humiliated, dear?" asked Cat.

At the moment Cat lay on her chaise lounge in her room, wrapped in her dressing robe, while Becky sat on the edge of the chair by the mantel. At Cat's words, Becky sat up even straighter.

"Will you be attentive for once in your life?" Becky snapped. "Lord Johnston is at this moment shut up in his chamber with a hot footbath, complaining of a dreadful chill from his dunking. Lady Ralston is lying down with a headache. Lord Rhodes is patiently observing our cousin Charles drink too much port in the library. I have no idea at all what is happening in Lord Weyland's household, but I hazard a guess it is a most awkward situation. How can it matter in the least if *I* am humiliated?"

Cat gazed at her pink-faced cousin, and at last sat up.

"I am so sorry, Becky. I did not mean to make you unhappy. But I have, haven't I?"

Becky sighed. "I am at long last mad. How is it that

you can incite me so much, and then make me forgive you in a moment? Madness is the only answer."

"You are a good and faithful friend, and I am thoughtless. That is the beginning and end of it."

"Not the end, I fear. Do not think the world will not be talking about your escapade. The better half of Hertfordshire was a witness to it. What will your father think? We must act quickly."

Cat turned her gaze out the casement windows.

Indeed, what would her father think? She knew he would not be concerned unless she ruined her reputation beyond redemption and rendered her "list" a useless bit of paper, filled with the names of English lords who would not marry her. But if she immediately became betrothed to an earl . . .

In her narrow view of the lawn through the window, a male peacock strutted into view, his tail feathers spread in full and pompous display.

"I think you mean I must marry quickly," Cat said.

"I think you should hope Lord Johnston is still willing."

A troublesome heaviness came to her chest. Cat rather wished that Lord Johnston would withdraw his suit. He seemed not, after all, to be the kind of gentleman who would let her do as she wished with no intrusion. He would not be . . . the sort of gentleman, for instance, that Lord Weyland would be.

Cat sighed. "I am certain my fortune has not lost its appeal. And if I am engaged without delay, the tittle-tattle about yesterday's little adventure will die soon enough."

"That is likely true, although Lord Johnston might not be wholly overjoyed. Happily, there is no provision on your list about your prospective husband being in love with you."

For the first time, something Becky said caused pain. Cat looked at Becky once more, and found she had no ability to put her thoughts into words. She was not quite sure why her feelings were in such tumult.

Becky blinked. "I meant to say . . . your list does not demand that *you* must be in love with your *husband*. So if Lord Johnston is your choice, you should wait no longer."

No, there was nothing to say she must be in love.

Cat gazed out the window again. Inside, she fortified her walls and drew upon her deep well of determination. Miss Catherine Prescott D'Eauville did not weep, nor did she surrender. Ever.

"There, Becky. I can always count upon you for a sensible opinion."

"Sensible? I?" Becky made a derisive sound. "I am daily grateful that *I* have no list."

Becky descended the main stair with a heavy heart. Cat appeared to be as determined as ever to maintain her current course—and in so doing, cause all manner of unhappiness including Cat's own. Naturally, Cat was not convinced of this, only Becky was. Cat, Becky thought, was like a kitten determined to drink milk from two saucers at once. She seemed incapable of giving up one thing to have the other, and so in the end would have neither.

Oh, Cat felt she would marry Lord Johnston *sometime*, Becky knew, but what Cat *wanted*, even if she did not realize it, was to continue to receive the attentions of Lord Weyland. Now this was out of the question—Lord Weyland had his Miss Millington, and Lord Johnston had a limited amount of patience. Even with pockets to let, Lord Johnston would quit the chase soon, particularly with Cat attempting to turn herself into the most recent Interesting Scandal. Another heiress would be considerably less trouble and do less damage to his reputation.

At least, this was Becky's conclusion, and she trusted

her opinion. A strong opinion was one thing she had much in common with her more spirited cousin.

Becky reached the bottom of the stairs before she admitted to herself the depth of her unhappiness. Lord Rhodes stood in the hall just outside Charles's study door, head bowed, apparently in contemplation of the tile at his feet. But even before she heard him sigh, Becky knew that his feeling was one of despair.

"My lord."

Lord Rhodes looked up and met her gaze. His eyes were heavy with gloom, but a spark of life flashed in them at the sight of her.

"Miss Prescott! My good, good Miss Prescott, whatever shall I do? I am the ruin of my family . . . quite undone. Miss D'Eauville will have none of me, it is plain, yet I should wonder if that is best! Still . . . I cannot say, for she is your cousin! Please forgive me . . ."

She reached him and touched his hand. "Lord Rhodes, come walk with me."

Still distracted, he let her take his arm and lead him to the doors to the garden. There they stepped out, and Becky led him along the flagstone path as far as the boxwood hedge before she spoke.

"Do not be afraid to speak to me of my cousin. I love her, but I also know her faults."

"I am ashamed. The fault is mine. I, and I alone, have allowed myself to come to this pass. To so desperately need to marry well and at all speed . . . there can be no question why Miss D'Eauville would not marry me, even if I do not wish to . . . that is . . ."

"Even if you do not wish to marry her? You may say it. I do understand. My cousin is a lovely person, so full of life, and yet not quite the one to fill the void in your children's lives."

"I . . . yes. That is it. A lovely person. But to be a wife to such as me . . ."

"She needs time. Our Miss D'Eauville is still learning of life."

"She is young. Oh, but my dear, dear Miss Prescott . . ." He stopped in the path and turned to her, taking both her hands. "You are as young, and yet . . . and yet . . . Forgive me! I have nothing to offer you! If only I had something besides penniless children and mortgaged walls! But if I were in the position . . . I would beg you . . . Oh, but I cannot say!"

Becky's heart turned over as she gazed into the soft brown eyes of her gentle, honorable Lord Rhodes. And then she heard herself say, "You need nothing to offer for me, my lord. Did you not know that I have a fortune of my own?"

His expression became one of astonishment. For a moment he seemed completely incapable of speech.

Becky licked her lips. "I am saying to you, Lord Rhodes, that you need not beg me to marry you. I shall, and quite willingly."

He sucked in a sharp breath. "Bless me! But . . . to marry you for your fortune, I cannot! Unthinkable!"

"You would not be marrying me for my fortune, my good sir. At least, that is my opinion of the matter. Can you disagree?"

"It is preposterous!" he cried. And then he kissed her.

Chapter Eleven

*I*t was just as well she had not known how hard this would be, Cat thought. If only she might go without a husband entirely—unfortunately, she could not.

Cat sat at her writing desk over her unfinished letter, gazing out her window at the late morning sky. Her casement was cracked open, for she liked the fresh air, and through it she heard the sound of a horse whicker. In the next moment she heard the distant call of a stable hand, then quiet once again.

She had no memory of her mother at all, but her father more than made up for that. With little imagination, she could feel him in her room at this moment, his great energy and resolve buoying her up in its forceful current. With little more effort, a long-ago memory sprang to life. She might have been twelve on the occasion she and her father first discussed her future.

> "Cat, my child, I am the most fortunate father alive to have you for my daughter. How can you wish to be a boy?"
>
> "But, Father, I do not want to be a daughter! I want to build ships."
>
> "As neither of us can make you a boy, there is no point in dwelling upon the matter. One chooses a battle one can win. You can do something no son of mine could do—marry a great English title and give me little

lords and ladies for grandchildren. My father—your grandfather—was Earl of Ralston. It is in our blood."

Cat had heard the story of her heritage many times, even then. Father had been a younger son, with no title and no fortune. He had come to America at the tender age of twenty-four, full of ambition, and married Miss Elizabeth Prescott, daughter of a wealthy shipbuilder.

"But who will run the shipyard if I go to England? I must stay here, Father."

"One of your Prescott cousins, like as not. No, I need you to go home to England, my dear. Yes, I think an earl would do very well for you. Certainly nothing less. You will have a great house and miles of beautiful park, and people will call you 'my lady.' You will be the toast of London."

"I do not want to be a toast of London. I want to be Cat and stay with you."

"Would you not wish to make me happy?"

At some point, Cat came to embrace her father's ambition as much as he did. She wanted to achieve her father's dream; she wanted him to be proud of her; and she resolved that after making her convenient marriage, she would travel the world and see all the places she had read of in books. Indeed, her father told her that this was a fine idea, and assured her he would make her in charge of her own purse as part of her marriage settlement. All in all, marrying an impoverished earl seemed a perfectly sensible, even an *agreeable*, plan.

Until now.

"Oh, fiddle," Cat said aloud. Staring out the window, she twirled her quill thoughtlessly until she broke the point against her page. Would Father object so very much to a mere baron as a son-in-law? Might Lord Weyland secretly desire her, or did he truly wish to marry Miss Millington? And when had Cat begun to consider the gentleman she married to be as important as her independence—or nearly as important, at least?

Suppose Miss Millington very much wished to marry Lord Weyland? Or had the engagement already been made?

Cat threw the useless quill, which fell short of the grate by some distance. "A fine thing!" she said to herself. "Certainly you cannot consider meddling with the engagement of another. Miss Catherine D'Eauville would never stoop to such an atrocious thing. Nor should she be required to!"

Cat stood up and strode distractedly across her chamber, turned at the mantel, and stalked back, her stride full of suppressed energy. She passed her writing desk and arrived at the side of her magnificent canopy bed. She turned again.

"I cannot break Father's heart," she muttered. "How difficult can it be to find oneself wed to Lord Johnston?"

He *was* handsome, she thought, and he had been wise enough to be quiet and not attempt to reprimand her after the adventure of the gypsies, even if he had tried to stop her. He might soak his feet in hot baths all day, and cover himself in mustard plasters all the night if he knew his place.

She took another step and stopped. "I must have air. My head is full of cobwebs." She swept around, snatched up her shawl from the chaise, and strode into the hall.

The garden air was refreshing. Cat drew in the early summer smells of honeysuckle and roses, for a few late roses were yet blooming at the bend in the flagstone path. The gentle breeze took her skirts and pressed them against her legs. She closed her eyes and inhaled deeply.

She wanted to dance alone in the grass, arms outstretched and body whirling round and round, as she had at home so long ago. She would smell the sea, hear the gulls' call, and turn and turn until she fell in a pile in a mass of billowing skirt and bare legs, for she would have shed the boots and stockings as soon as she had escaped the watchful eye of Nanny Jane. But she was no longer at Father's great Boston home at the edge of the sea, and she was no longer a child.

No.

Cat dashed a single tear away and opened her eyes. The lovely English garden surrounded her, with its pruned elegance and noble grace. And Cat longed for the wild thicket and the untamed sea grasses, and the time when there was nothing between her soul and the sky but her dreams.

She was not free.

But it was not good to think in this way. Catherine Prescott D'Eauville did not cry. She was her father's wonderful, strong, spirited daughter, and he had sacrificed his life making her a wealthy young woman. However her heart turned, whatever turmoil came within her, Father's happiness was the goal of all her efforts. Her reward, she had long ago determined, was fair indeed. She would be an independent woman and possess the kind of freedom most females could only wish for.

She walked slowly, turning matters over in her mind. The answer, clearly, was to wed Lord Johnston. But why *would* her heart be so heavy at the thought?

She came to the bend in the path, walked slowly around it, and stopped.

Ahead of her, under the boughs of a sheltering apple tree, two figures embraced. She gazed at them in surprise, not believing whom it was she saw.

Her dear Becky, and Lord Rhodes.

Cat's feet would not move. Her mind could not will her body to respond. She could only look upon the form of her faithful, wise, gentle Becky in love.

The kiss ended tenderly, and Becky stood gazing up into the eyes of her Lord Rhodes. Then she turned her head, as if she sensed something, and her eyes met Cat's.

Becky's eyes widened, and she looked stricken. She drew breath. "I must explain. You see, we are to be married."

Cat found her voice. It came out oddly expressionless. "You need explain nothing to me. I wish you happy."

"Yes, I *must* explain. Dear Cat, I . . . Lord Rhodes and I . . . decided that we have feelings for each other. And, I admit, we neither of us expected this to happen."

Her Becky was in love with Lord Rhodes. How and when had this happened? Why hadn't Cat known?

Here Lord Rhodes found his tongue, although his face was flushed and his eyes seemed not to know where to go. "Miss D'Eauville . . . I hope . . . that is, I entreat . . . The devil, I have made a muddle of things!"

He was a sweet man, and Cat took pity on him. "You need say nothing, only agree to take good care of my Becky. I sincerely, deeply, wish you both well."

And then Cat found herself turned around on the path, her feet leading her blindly back toward Ralston Hall.

Cat's world had irreversibly changed. Her sensible, loyal Becky had done the unthinkable—and left her all on her own.

Cat climbed the steps from the garden, crossed the veranda and opened the door to the inside hall. Immediately she came face-to-face, nose-to-nose with Lady Ralston, and stopped barely in time.

Susan laughed. By each hand she held one of her children, little Margaret and young William. Behind followed the harried nurse.

"There you are, my dear Miss D'Eauville! We were just on our way into the garden. I had thought you not yet down. Lord Johnston wishes to speak with you."

The words struck her through like a thunderbolt. *Lord Johnston wishes to speak with you.*

Ah, there was the reason for Lady Ralston's high spirits. All now anticipated a wedding instead of a scandal. Cat might have found it all very amusing if her head was not in such turmoil.

"Then he must be recovered from his wetting. I am very glad. If you should see him, please be certain to tell him so."

From the nearby door into Lord Ralston's study, Lord Johnston himself just then stepped into the hall. "You may tell him yourself," he said to Cat. He smiled his warm, handsome smile. "May I please speak with you alone for a moment, Miss D'Eauville?"

All turned and gazed at Lord Johnston, and even young William and little Margaret were wide-eyed in expectation, looking first at Lord Johnston, then at Cat, then back at Lord Johnston.

Cat blinked. She felt curiously numb. Then she extended her hand. "Very well."

Lord Johnston took her hand and led her into the small sitting room across the way. Closing the door behind them, he turned and took both of her hands in his.

"My dearest Miss D'Eauville, you must know how I feel. I dare to hope that you feel the same. Will you make me the happiest man alive and become my wife?"

Cat gazed up into his handsome face, into his handsome dark eyes. She should be swooning if she were a natural young woman, she supposed. But she wished his eyes were gray and not brown.

"I must say I do not know how you feel," she said. A feeling of strange calm overtook her. "I am a woman who likes her own way. I shall not change. I have distressed you in the short time we have known each other. I *will* not have you mislead."

Lord Johnston blinked. "Yes . . . er, I realize . . . that you are . . . a unique, exciting woman." He swallowed. "I am unchanged. Will you say yes?"

Cat felt her heart slow. A hope, like a snowflake, melted and vanished.

"Yes, I shall." She withdrew her hands. "We shall speak more later, shall we?"

Stepping around a bewildered Lord Johnston, she re-entered the hallway to find Lady Ralston, the nurse, little Margaret, and young William still gathered there. Instantly, all talk ceased, and all of them gazed at her. Lady Ralston appeared to be holding her breath.

"I may as well tell it at once," Cat said. "Lord Johnston has asked me to marry him, and I have said yes. So now I must add a line or two to my father's letter." She started for the stairs, then paused. She looked back at the group of watchers, which now included Lord Johnston.

Lord Johnston, she felt, appeared to be relieved. Perversely, she searched his face briefly, but she could not identify a more tender emotion. She wondered, in fact, whether his look might be better described as resigned.

Cat picked up her chin. "Oh, as I am acting as bearer of tidings, when you go into the garden, offer your congratulations to the couple you find there. We have an excess of joy today, it seems."

Lord Weyland found himself uncharacteristically out of sorts. It was in part due to the fact that he had been subject to Mr. Millington's intrusive company for the past several days, while Mrs. Millington took up all of his aunt Beatrice's time in the drawing room, and Miss Millington spent the bulk of her days, he had on good authority, crying her eyes out in her room. These were not circumstances to soothe the temper of a thinking man.

He managed at last to make an escape some three days after the bridge and gypsy debacle, leaving Mr. Millington asleep on a chaise in the library, and went out riding with his trusty writing box and his faithful Boofus bounding behind him. He found putting his thoughts in order on paper a soul-soothing exercise, and he guided his horse straight to a favorite spot nestled in a copse of trees. Here it opened into a tiny clearing, and today there was a spot of sun filtering through the leaves.

Lord Weyland dismounted, spread his coat on the ground beneath a sturdy oak, and sat with a sigh, his back resting against the trunk. He watched his hound investigate the scents of their resting spot, and when Boofus trotted off in pursuit of an unknown creature, Jack closed his eyes, listening to the silence and feeling the breath of wind on his face. It was a blessed relief; and for some time he sat there, simply feeling the peace.

Ah, such a turmoil as his life was now in! From his former charmed state, how had this turn come about? He had done nothing to bring it upon himself. Now fate seemed determined to wrest his single state from him, or leave him forever miserable.

He was still mildly annoyed with his aunt for encouraging the visit of the Millingtons, although he had to acquit her of malice. She had only extended the invitation, and that she had done some months before. Jack believed, in truth, that the Millingtons had not determined to come until the end of their daughter's unremarkable first Season in London.

Still, if not for the world-shaking Miss D'Eauville, he would have been his usual courteous self, and soon seen the end of the Millingtons' visit with no unhappiness on either side. He might, indeed, have finally decided to make his aunt's dearest wish come true and asked for Miss Millington's hand. Perhaps. It had occurred to him of late that he might consider marriage before he was too old. He was still forming his opinions on the matter.

In any case, his present circumstances were not happy ones . . . not since the fateful day at the old bridge, when he had ferried the fair Miss D'Eauville across the Wye. Now he must determine what to do.

At last, he opened his small lap desk, withdrew paper and his writing instruments, and began to compose.

*A man reaches a point in his career where he
must decide whether or not to marry. The list is
long in favor of continuing the single state for a
man who has enough in the way of fortune and
interests to maintain himself happily. However,
there are certain factors that weigh with him
which encourage him to give thought to matrimony.
The wishes of members of his close family may
be one of those, in addition to his own thoughts of
his mortality.*

*In any case, let us say he has reached that point
in his considerations.*

Here Lord Weyland stopped, blotted his sheet, and
withdrew another page from his writing desk.

*The question then becomes, rather than whether
he should marry at all, but whom shall he marry?
And might he do himself a better turn by falling
upon his sword?*

He paused, admiring his turn of words. That only
occupied him for the barest moment before he returned
to the issue at hand.

*A man might easily choose a wife who is decora-
tive and to the main purpose rather than a comfort in any other way. As there are other sources of
pleasure and companionship to any intelligent
man, a wife may not be expected to provide for all.
Wisest of all is perhaps to expect a wife to provide
as little as possible.*

He thought of Miss Millington. Regardless of outward purpose, he knew the Millingtons hoped to make
a match between their daughter and himself. It was all,
of course, something of a disaster. Miss Millington, he
felt quite certain, had been cast into an ill humor due
to his supposed fondness for Miss D'Eauville. This had

prompted the Millingtons to advocate even more stren-
uously on her behalf, ultimately driving him to hide
today from their parental hooks and snares.

He could not choose Miss D'Eauville, of course, who
now held his interest in every way possible, for in addition to her own objections to marrying *him*, to wed her
would be to destitute his friend Charles. Perhaps he
might better propose to Miss Millington, whose expectations had been built so high, and have the thing done
with.

*A man might also choose a woman who enslaves
his very senses, and robs him of his soul. All
reason demands that he set her aside for a wife who
would take but an ordinary place in his life and
leave him with some semblance of his honor and
his wits.*

Lord Weyland leaned his head back against the
sturdy trunk of oak and closed his eyes once more. The
soft wind brushed his face and riffled the leaves above,
ebbing and flowing and ebbing again like the very
breath of the earth.

She was beautiful. There was no woman like her in
his experience . . . tall and strong and lovely, full of
vitality and fecundity. Her mind was clever; her laughter was music. If he could but hold her in his arms, he
imagined he would feel heaven itself. But the devil of
it was, she was so very much more willful than any
angel. . . .

And his lordship fell fast asleep.

"Father, I have accepted Lord Johnston. Now I wish
to the very devil I could speak with you and have your
opinion." Cat made her conversation with the wind as
she guided her mare across the verge of parkland and
field. It was not a good thing that she should feel such

an urgent need to communicate; it indicated that she was unsettled, uncertain, and it was a state she hated.

"He is on The List. He is a gentleman, an earl, and amenable to my wishes, for the most part. I should think he would serve both our purposes well enough."

Cat gave the mare her head and allowed her to walk where she would while Cat continued to wage the battle in her mind. She was aware that the sky was a beautiful azure this early afternoon, the grasses a shimmering green, the air laden with the freshness of summer bloom. She could not, however, feel any interest in those things. She was too distracted by a kind of heaviness in her breast.

Becky had looked so happy when she had seen her last. There had been so many smiles, so much laughter over dinner the previous night. Cousin Charles had given a delighted toast to the couple; Cousin Susan had expressed her joy again and again; and Lord Rhodes, once so somber and sorrowful, smiled as she had never seen him smile. Then, when she had noticed their hands clasp in genuine affection, she had felt . . . so alone.

Becky was of an age and situation to consent to marriage for herself; Cat's own engagement had not been formally announced, given she had not yet her father's approval. But Cat's feelings had nothing to do with the delay, for all knew her father's consent would come. The smiles of Charles and Susan were as much for Lord Johnston and herself as they were for dear Becky and Lord Rhodes.

It was a foolish thought, but Cat found herself searching for any reason her father might say no. She could find none.

How strange is fate, she thought. *That I have spent half my life wishing for what is about to take place, so my life might go on and Father be happy, and now I believe I do not want it at all.*

A moment later she thought that fate was stranger still. First, she spotted a flicker of white in the corner of her eye just as her mare shied. Quickly and skillfully she brought her mount under control, and had just time enough to see that the object of terror was a piece of white vellum caught in the brush near an outcropping of woods. Curiosity overcame practicality, and she dismounted.

The paper appeared to be fresh and untouched by rain. Leading her mare, Cat started for her object.

Then she heard the murmured voices from within the copse.

Chapter Twelve

"*I* despise you!" The young woman sobbed. There was a brief moment, and then her voice came again, muffled this time. "No . . . I wish . . . I wish we had met long ago . . . long before *she* came!"

"Please, dearest . . . do not cry. There is no help for it; you know there is not."

Cat stood very still by her horse, screened from the lovers' sight by the intervening trees. She dared not move for fear of discovery; of course, she could not help but overhear everything that was said.

There was a moment of silence, and the rustling of cloth. Cat pictured the couple clinging together in an attempt to comfort each other.

She heard the young woman sniff. "I do not care about Weyland's silly fortune! I have money enough for us both. You do not need that—that American! Oh, why did you ask for her? Why . . ."

"Hush, darling. Hush." There was a pause. "Hear me. I am at the edge of ruin. I stand to lose my property without immediate financial relief. Miss D'Eauville's father understands my problem, but your father would very likely dismiss me, no matter what my title! Why would he not, with Lord Weyland's fortune to choose? You know I have no choice but to marry Miss D'Eauville."

Miss Millington. And my eyes—Lord Johnston.

"But I do not know it! We might have spoken to my father!"

"Listen, my love. What sort of gentleman would I be to thoughtlessly court one woman, then another? If my title were enough to interest your father, my behavior would repel him. If that were not sufficient, there is the matter of Miss D'Eauville's reputation. After her behavior at the picnic, it behooves me to marry her without delay."

"I cannot think how you can marry her at all!"

"Hush, darling. In a single lady her wild flights might be shocking, but once a countess, they might be but winked at. And I must marry her regardless."

Wild flights!

"I shall die without you!"

"No, you shall not die. We will never forget each other. I shall always remember that happy day when we met by the old bridge. I will never forget your gentle hands administering the cloth to my head . . ."

Aha . . . I begin to see.

". . . and holding my cup of wine while I lay wet and miserable! But you will find yourself happy again bye and by."

"Never . . . never . . . I shall have to marry Lord Weyland, and he treats me as the merest child, and I will never be happy again!"

Cat stayed motionless, a strange feeling stealing over her. It was definitely disturbing . . . yes, it was an injury to her pride. The strong, confident, assured Miss D'Eauville had been rendered a completely unexpected blow. It was one thing not to passionately love one's espoused, but quite another if one's espoused was attached to someone else. Particularly, when the injured party was herself!

It was clear to a fool that Lord Johnston had charmed the young Miss Millington, and that Miss Millington was in love with him. It was quite possible that Lord Johnston loved Miss Millington as well.

"You must go," Lord Johnston said. "You have been absent too long."

Miss Millington's reply was muffled. Then, presently, Cat heard the sound of horses departing.

"The cad!" Cat fumed. Cat may have wanted a convenient marriage, but she had expected her future husband's constancy. But as she thought on this, she realized that she was doing Lord Johnston an injustice. It seemed that he and Miss Millington had come together in circumstances of Cat's own doing; and now he was doing the most one could expect of a gentleman . . . he was telling Miss Millington good-bye.

Another feeling rose within her then—sympathy. Miss Millington was not, after all, in control of her parents' actions or of Lord Johnston's. Miss Millington was as much a victim as Cat. And . . . Cat felt another stab of unhappiness for herself. Johnston was marrying her out of duty as much as for her money. In parcel with that insult, she alone seemed to be the only one unable to be loved!

What a fine pickle it all was! Cat had accepted Lord Johnston, who loved and was loved by Miss Millington, whom the Millingtons were throwing at Lord Weyland's head, who was very possibly on his way to requesting Miss Millington's hand. Cat could not delight in *that* prospect—particularly now that she knew Miss Millington loved Lord Johnston! What should an intelligent woman do at this juncture?

Still debating, Cat's gaze found again the sheet of paper in the shrubbery. She reached for it.

The paper proved to be a piece of thick vellum, freshly written upon. Cat plucked it carefully from its thorny prison. She recognized the hand, and her heart sped up. She lost no time in scanning Lord Weyland's words.

"A man might also choose a woman who enslaves his very senses, and robs him of his soul . . ."

"Oho!" she murmured. "Truth, you are mine!" Cat smiled softly to herself. She had her answer. An intelligent woman would interfere in the present course of events—and she was quite definitely an intelligent woman!

As quickly as it came, her smile faded. *Father. The*

List. Oh, bother it all! Somehow, she would manage it. She was certain she would find a way. Clutching the expensive vellum securely in her gloved hand, she turned back to her mare.

She could not mount, of course. Cat glanced about for a serviceable object to use as a step, but neither stone nor log presented itself.

"Silly goose," she said aloud. She might have known that her ability to lose her groom would eventually land her in difficulties. Fortunately, she was used to walking, and was shod to do so. Leading her mare, she set forth to find a suitable spot to mount.

It took a half hour of walking steadily, up hill and down, and Cat was soon overheated. At last she made her way down the hedgerow to another copse of trees, and then led her horse within. But what was this? She stopped stock-still. Abandoned lap desk by his side, Lord Weyland lay asleep beneath a tree, his faithful hound curled up beside him.

Opportunity had never knocked more loudly upon her door. Or, perhaps, it was fate.

Cat watched. There he was, his coat was unbuttoned, his long legs stretched out before him, and his head turned slightly to the side so she could see his face. His hat lay beside him in the grass, his hair was tousled, and his eyelashes seemed very dark and thick against his skin. He looked so . . . so very innocent.

Cat had had no prior occasion in her life to see a man sleep. But she knew that if she had, it would have seemed considerably different than watching *Lord Weyland* now.

A warmth curled up inside her and hummed softly, like a kitten's purr. Lord Weyland was such a very . . . *lovely* man. There was something about his strong English features that drew her, while Lord Johnston's perfection of face did not. And she very much wanted to creep up to him and tuck that wayward curl of hair back from his eyes.

She wanted, God help her, to trace the shape of his lips with her fingertip.

Cat stared at the resting Lord Weyland while the warmth rose in her cheeks. What she was feeling, she was certain, was passion. She had certainly seen it before, but never believed that she felt it herself. It was a surprising thing. A marvelous thing. It took over her rational mind and turned it into a . . . oh, drat, she had no words for it. Her ability to think was truly gone.

Boofus awoke and raised his great rough gray head. Cat extended her hand gently and made a soft comforting sound, and recognition flashed over the hound's face. He came eagerly to his feet and sidled up to her, wiggling with devotion, and Cat scratched behind his ears.

Father, forgive me. She drew a slow breath, straightened her shoulders, and walked up to the sleeping gentleman.

Lord Weyland slapped mildly at the marauding fly. For a moment the irritating tickle on his nose was gone; then it was back. He swatted again, and his fingers struck a strangely displaced stalk of grass. He snapped his eyes open.

He did not think he was dreaming. He believed he was quite awake, lying beneath a tree. However, standing over him was the figure of Miss D'Eauville, only from his perspective she appeared a veritable giantess. His gaze traveled up her emerald braid and frog-trimmed riding dress, up over her very distinctive bosom, to her elegant cocked head. Perhaps he was dreaming still?

Then his vision spoke. "And so I descend upon your marvelous escape. Are you refreshed?" she asked. She bent and, extending her hand, twitched the stem of grass over his nose. Then she straightened and smiled.

Jack blinked. No, it was truly Miss D'Eauville. Rubbing his nose, he sat up and gazed into her dancing eyes.

"My dear Miss D'Eauville, a gentleman will always tell a lady that he is refreshed upon sight of her."

She laughed. "What craft men use. I wonder if I should trust a single thing you say." She then withdrew her other hand from behind her back—and dangled a piece of vellum from her gloved fingertips. "I do hope you do not *fall upon your sword* on my behalf."

Could it be . . . ? Jack looked quickly at his writing desk beside him. The top of it was bare. A short distance away, one of the sheets he had written upon lay caught in grass, riffling in the mild breeze. *The devil.*

He composed himself and turned back to her. Of course, there was his traitorous hound lying adoringly at her feet.

"Miss D'Eauville . . . I suppose it would be of no use to say that I had certain expectations of my writing being private."

"That is right, it would be of no use at all. Tell me, am I merely decorative and to the main purpose, or do I enslave your senses and steal your soul? I am not certain I like the choice. I had thought that I accomplished all."

She was very happy in teasing him, he saw. And, the devil of it was, he enjoyed it.

He decided it was time to eliminate Miss D'Eauville's unusual advantage of height, and climbed to his feet. Gazing into her lively, lovely face, he said, "I believe it would do me no good to admit to, or to deny, either. You have already drawn your conclusion."

For a moment her expression clouded. Then the smile returned. "You are right. I have. And so I must ask . . . will you marry Miss Millington?"

The grove seemed to grow still around him. Suddenly he was overly warm—where had the breeze gone?

Jack cleared his throat. "Er—Miss Millington and I— that is to say, the Millingtons and my aunt—oh, bother it." He stopped to gather his wits and felt her eyes intent on his face.

"Are Miss Millington and yourself engaged to be married?"

"No."

"Excellent!"

"But the possibility suggests itself. The Millingtons are acquainted with the family, and my aunt is anxious for me to establish myself, although it is no urgent desire of mine—"

"But there is no engagement. There have been no promises made."

Jack drew a steadying breath. Miss D'Eauville was certainly his match today, and his enjoyment of their banter was fast approaching fear.

"That is true. My aunt acquiesced to the Millingtons' visit—it was rather precipitous, you understand. They are looking for a solid husband for their daughter."

"They are looking for *you* for their daughter."

"I—well, yes. But there has been no understanding, as I said. However, I have been giving thought . . ."

Miss D'Eauville's large brown eyes remained locked to his face, and not a hint of a smile remained on her lips. Her very body seemed still and listening. He felt suddenly light-headed.

"You have been giving thought?" she asked.

There they stood, face-to-face beneath the oak, he and a fascinating, beautiful woman; but Jack felt paralyzed, as though a dangerous beast cornered him. He had once compared her to Medusa. Perhaps she *had* turned him into stone.

"I am nearly nine and twenty," he said.

Cat blinked. Jack stood tall before her, but with all of his English reserve, his expression was more vulnerable than she had ever seen it. He was an arm's length away, but she could feel him; she could, as surely as if their bodies were touching.

He loved her. She knew it. He loved her.

She tilted her head and attempted an arch expression. "Before the arrival of Miss Millington, I seem to remem-

ber a sentiment about marriage and dancing for the
queen, with your preference in favor of the queen."
She hesitated. "But I do not believe you are in love
with her."

"I . . . of course I love the queen."

Cat burst into a laugh. It was so silly, so foolish, and
so . . . important. But she was laughing, and she saw
that he was suddenly smiling as well.

"Touché, my good gentleman. No, of course I mean
that you are not in love with Miss Millington. You may
seal your lips if you wish; but if you do not deny this,
I shall know that it is true."

"Miss D'Eauville . . ." His expression was serious
once more. "I know that your rapid thoughts have lead
you to some conclusion. Perhaps you might share it
with me."

Cat had never felt so giddy or afraid. She, afraid!
Once it was not to be thought of. But somehow, now,
she found herself floundering in an abyss of confusion
she had thought reserved for all other mortals.

"Very well." Cat raised her chin. "Lord Johnston has
proposed to me, and I have said yes. But I believe I
should alter my decision." She paused. "I should like
your advice on the matter."

Sad. His eyes looked sad. There he stood, bareheaded,
neckerchief askew, and a new breeze brought her the
scent of his perspiration mingled with light cologne. He
would not say what she wished to hear.

"It would be best," he said quietly, "that you marry
Lord Johnston."

Cat took in a deep breath. She was nearly trembling.
Absurd! But she felt a quaking from the center of her
being.

"And for what reason? I do not believe that you are
the least concerned with my little visit with gypsies. If
you cannot object to marrying me, and you are not in love
with Miss Millington, what can the matter possibly be?"

He hesitated only a brief moment. "I am only a baron, and I am too rich."

"I have changed my mind on my requirements. I am as entitled to a change of mind as you are."

"I should boss you about horribly. I should forever be dithering around who knows where with my research and studies. I know your feelings about financially independent men. Why, I should be impossible."

More perspiration had appeared on Lord Weyland's forehead. He looked as near to desperate as he could appear. But he *did* love her. She knew this. He was afraid.

"Come. If I do not wish to marry Lord Johnston, it should be of no consequence to you. It is I who will have to soften Father's disappointment, after all. Let us marry, and I promise not to rob you of all of your wits."

"Miss D'Eauville . . ." Lord Weyland withdrew his handkerchief and dabbed his brow. Pocketing it once more, he met her gaze squarely. Now, she saw resolve in his eyes. Her heart plunged.

"You must marry Lord Johnston . . . or another earl, it does not matter. Your cousin's fortune and fate depend upon it."

"I beg your pardon?"

"Charles has an agreement with your father."

Cat stood stunned. In all of her imaginings, such a possibility had never occurred to her. "Agreement? What sort of agreement?"

Lord Weyland's expression remained immobile. "A sum of money will be provided to Charles when you secure a match that your father approves. Miss D'Eauville, your cousin will face ruin if you do otherwise. He is deeply in debt." He paused and drew breath. "And I, as his very old and loyal friend . . . I cannot be the means by which he is destroyed."

Chapter Thirteen

*F*or perhaps the first time in her life, Cat was speechless. Lord Weyland's words were as unexpected as they were painful. Emotions churned within her, too raw to be named. But over all, she did understand this one thing: that Father had not trusted her marriage decision to her alone.

His desire that she marry an impressive title had always mattered greatly to her. Breaking his heart was terrible to contemplate, and she had not considered this possibility lightly. But her father had sought to *insure* that she followed his will, without regard to her own desires, intelligence, or happiness.

"Miss D'Eauville . . . I apologize deeply. I dislike very much giving you pain. I wished it had not been necessary to tell you this."

Cat found her tongue. "You know of my father's and Charles's agreement from Charles, I presume?"

"Yes."

"And who else knows of this?"

"I do not know."

"For how long have you had this information that was, apparently, not intended for my ears?"

"Charles informed me the afternoon of the ball."

Cat straightened her shoulders. Gazing up into Lord Weyland's serious gray eyes, she determined that she would not show him one hint of weakness. "Oh, well.

I suppose I should be grateful that you have been truthful with me."

He blinked. "You would not have believed anything other," he said quietly. "Miss D'Eauville, I have the greatest respect for your good sense."

"Of course I would not believe anything but the truth," she snapped. "Not when I have seen *this*!" She waved the vellum sheet beneath his nose, then, with an imperious twitch of her wrist, released it so it floated gently to the ground at his feet. "Not that it is any consequence *why* you will not marry me. I wish you well, Lord Weyland. I shall leave you with a piece of advice—I suggest you do not wed Miss Millington. Good day." She turned and began toward her mare, which stood patiently some distance away. Every step seemed a gigantic effort. Foolishly, she knew, she had wanted him to admit that he loved her, and he had not. Of course, he *would* not, if he could not marry her.

She arrived at the horse. Belatedly, she recalled the reason she was not mounted.

Annoyed with herself, Cat turned back to Lord Weyland. He stood where she had left him, quietly gazing after her.

"I require assistance," Cat said. "If you please."

He nodded, then walked slowly toward her. "I thought as much."

She became aware of her heart, of her breathing, both laboring as if she had sprinted a short distance rather than walked. She held his gaze as he drew closer, standing straight and tall, telling him with her eyes that she was perfectly equal to the situation. A whisper in her mind suggested that she was not.

He stopped before her. Behind her she felt the solid warmth of her mare; he subtly braced her from the front, even though he stood an arm's length away.

"At your service, Miss D'Eauville," he said gently. "But might you indulge me first by telling me why I should not marry Miss Millington?"

She caught her breath and gazed into his eyes. There she saw something in their depths, cloaked though it was.

She was not mistaken, no, she was not! He had feelings for her, the proper Lord Weyland. He would go to his death defending duty and honor if he must, but he could not disguise the truth from her.

But here was a dilemma. Miss Millington's heart was not Cat's secret to reveal. And certainly, if Cat were required to marry Lord Johnston, Cat did not wish to divulge his *affaire de la coeur* with Miss Millington—particularly to Lord Weyland. Ah, pride! She possessed more than her share of it.

"She is too young."

"She is old enough, it seems."

"Not for you."

"What? You would have me bowlegged and gray at eight and twenty?"

"Do not be absurd. It is your age relative to hers."

"And I suppose your own age is of no consequence."

Cat straightened her shoulders. "I am two and twenty."

"I now see."

"Do not attempt to make fun of me, Lord Weyland. Miss Millington is eighteen at most and very inexperienced. I am quite different, and well you know it."

His eyes narrowed slightly. "Do I?"

"If you do not, then you have not the perception I thought you possessed."

"And if *you* are wrong about my perception, might that say something of your own discernment?"

Cat drew a shaky breath. The man was driving her quite mad. He stood so close, and stared at her in such a way, and persisted in bandying words with her, when all she wanted from him was to assist her to mount her horse!

She wanted nothing more of him. Surely, she did not.

"You are purposely being difficult. My understanding is quite strong, I assure you."

"In fact, it is not your understanding, but your experience that I question. There are ways, Miss D'Eauville, in which Miss Millington and yourself are very similar."

Surely if she did not mount and ride away immediately, something unprecedented would happen. She felt it prickling her awareness, like the strange silence of birdsong before a storm. But . . . she did not want to ride away. She wanted to stay here on the ground, face-to-face with Lord Weyland, and confront whatever it was that beckoned. Miss Catherine Prescott D'Eauville could do nothing less.

Cat raised her chin, took one step forward, and waggled an admonishing finger below Lord Weyland's nose.

"Now you have become entirely absurd. You have eaten something bad, or you are intoxicated, or you have your king's disease. There is *nothing* similar between Miss Millington and myself."

He blinked and focused on the accusing finger beneath his nose, but did not move nor flinch.

"Kiss me," she said.

"Er—what?"

With great satisfaction, she saw that she had truly taken him off his guard. His eyes showed pure astonishment. She lowered her finger. "Do I shock you? Well, do not fret. I wish to distinguish myself from Miss Millington—that is all. You will not be required to marry me."

"Miss D'Eauville, I—"

Miss Catherine Prescott D'Eauville threw her arms around Lord Weyland's neck and kissed him.

Or rather . . . she aimed at his lips with hers and credibly found her target. In that moment the thrill of adventure coursed through her veins. As she pushed herself up and against him, Cat felt his body stiffen and his hard shoulders tense beneath her arms. His lips remained immobile as she pressed her mouth harder against them. She might have been attempting to kiss a tree.

Just once. She needed him to kiss her, just once.

Then his lips softened, and in the same instant his body became pliant. His arms came around her. He touched her lips with his tongue. Cat melted.

So *this* was a kiss. It was the sun on her face, it was the scent of rain on spring violets. It was the joy of morning and the lingering caress of the evening wind. It was the magnificent sea that lifted her ship and carried her beneath a saffron moon. It left no room for anything else to be felt.

She was lost, lost. And she remained so until she became aware of a gloved hand cupping her face, and the sudden cool caress of the breeze on her damp lips where his warm mouth had been. She opened her eyes.

Lord Weyland's strong, handsome face looked down into hers, his expression solemn, his gray eyes troubled.

"Miss D'Eauville," he said softly, "it is exactly as I suspected . . . and I am a cad exemplar. Please forgive me."

Cat blinked, digesting this turn of events. Her body yet tingled from the kiss, and if he released his hold on her, she was uncertain she would remain standing.

His words became meaning to her. "As you suspected? And quite what were you expecting? I do not feel I like that opinion." She drew her arms away from his neck, and as his hands dropped away from her, she stepped back. Her legs came up against a large canine obstacle.

"I hazard that you did not find me similar to Miss Millington," she said loftily. Boofus, ignoring her regal posture, thrust his nose worshipfully under her hand.

"Miss D'Eauville . . ." Lord Weyland reached out one hand halfheartedly, then dropped it back to his side. He sighed. It was a dismal, and very discouraging, sound. "No. I do not find you like Miss Millington. Not in the least."

She caught a deep breath, and was surprised to find that it staunched a sob. He was not at all reacting the way she had hoped. He was attempting to soothe her, she knew it—in spite of how he felt. She was certain she knew how he felt!

What was happening to her? It was all wrong. Everyone was being compelled to do as they did not wish to do, save Becky and Lord Rhodes. They . . . they alone were happy.

They—and perhaps Boofus, who pressed his great head hopefully against her thigh.

"Thank you," she said stiffly. "Would you please now help me to mount?"

It was over in the blink of an eye. Lord Weyland received her booted foot in his hands and tossed her, lightly and expertly, onto her mare. She adjusted the reins and gazed down at him. "Shall we see you at dinner?"

His hesitation told her before his words did. "My guests will dine at home with my aunt and me tonight. Perhaps in a few evenings' time." He paused, his steady gaze holding her eyes. "We must not meet again this way," he said. "I am sincerely sorry for my behavior in this."

Cat lifted her chin and gazed aloofly down her nose at him. "So am I . . . but not for the reason you suppose. Good-bye."

She urged her horse, and set course for home. She did not look back.

"How is it possible," Cat said to herself, *"that I could have made such a colossal error?"* She urged her mare relentlessly on at a fast pace, desiring to put as much distance between herself and the unaccommodating Lord Weyland as possible.

Her father had secretly conspired to control her fate.

Cousin Charles had concealed the truth from her. Lord Johnston had deceived her. And Lord Weyland—he had refused her! It was all too much to accept. But accept it, she must. Miss Catherine Prescott D'Eauville would not hide from the truth, no matter how painful. She had been roundly taken in. And, she had been quite, quite wrong.

What to do now was at issue here, and nothing else, she told herself. But where the old Cat would have shoved away inconvenient feelings with firm resolve, today she found her thoughts completely topsy-turvy. They chased each other around and around in circles like spring kittens, never finding resolution, only more pursuit. No logical course presented itself that she could bring herself to adopt. She had never wanted something so much in her life before that would bring so much pain to others.

What she *wanted* was to marry Lord Weyland, a gentleman who was not on her blasted list.

She had not truly considered it before, but here was a man with a will as strong as her own—no, perhaps stronger. For truth to tell, when his desire conflicted with his duty, his need to follow duty was even greater than hers. And now, strangely, compellingly, this attracted her more than her old conviction that she must always hold the upper hand.

Of course, she had never experienced such a conflict between desire and duty before—not in many years, not since her earliest girlhood. She had since formed her desires to conform to her duty, and now that all was overset, she did not clearly know how to go on.

There was yet another thing that she had never before considered—that her fortune was not under her own control. Her generous allowance in itself was not nearly enough to assist her cousin Charles out of his financial crisis. And Father . . . her father was not concerned with the fate of Charles and his family, Cat knew. Father had ever resented his status as younger son, and would consider that his nephew Charles had brought his woes upon himself.

She might refuse to marry Lord Johnston, but if she married a gentleman of lesser status—if she could convince Lord Weyland to marry her—Father would allow Charles to be ruined. He might even deny her a dowry to ensure it. It would be quite bad enough to deal with Father's disappointment alone.

Poor Charles . . . and poor Father. How could she be happy when her happiness meant the ruin of theirs? But if she at present felt no particular sympathy with Lord Johnston, there was poor little Miss Millington's fate to be thought of in this confusion of alliances. And how could Cat bear marrying anyone but Lord Weyland?

Cat was in this state of mind when she looked at last across the park at her approach to Ralston Hall. From her angle she had a view of the circular drive, and saw by the appearance of a carriage that new visitors had arrived. Her interest perked immediately, and she urged her mare to a faster pace. She would think of something, and perhaps the key might be found among the new arrivals.

Cat rode into the stable yard, mood restored, and smiled broadly at the redheaded groom who came running. "Hello, Timothy-Thomas!" She brought her mare to a halt near him. "I see we have more visitors. Had you heard who they might be?" She looked across the yard at the carriage, which was still at a stand in front of Ralston Hall. At the moment three menservants were struggling to unload a large chest from the boot.

"Beg pardon, miss. I don' know. It is a hired rig."

Cat looked back at the boy, still smiling. "Well, it is a pity you do not know more."

"I know sommat more. 'E is from America."

"What did you say?"

"Er . . ." The boy gulped. "I . . . I *think* 'e is from America, miss. He is a right tall gentlemun, he is, with a big boomin' voice. He sounds like a Yankee, sum-mat." He blushed. "Er . . . that is . . . 'e sounds like a fine gent . . . like you. But you are a fine lady. From America."

Cat's heart squeezed into a tight little ball. Of course. Father was here.

Lord Weyland grabbed up his papers, shoved them into his lap desk willy-nilly, and mounted his dozing horse. In a flash, he and his startled mount were heading for home, with the oblivious Boofus loping behind.

To think he had allowed it to happen! What a ghastly idiot he was! He had kissed the sublime Miss D'Eauville, and in that one fell blow he had exhibited asinine disrespect for both Miss D'Eauville and Miss Millington. At his age—his *extreme* maturity, according to Miss D'Eauville—he should know what he was about! But no, he had exposed all to shame and pain, including himself.

This was an impossible situation. Impossible, and untenable. Of course his circumstances could not be both impossible and untenable, for he was surely living with the mess he'd made—so that would make it both possible *and* tenable. Oh, yes! How comforting it was to find accurate words to describe his debacle! He'd be certain to write *that* in his journal, and send it right off to the curious Miss D'Eauville!

Lord Weyland rode up to his stable in a dervish of whirling thoughts, and his boy Thomas appeared as if conjured from the shadows of the barn.

"You will walk him," Jack snapped as he dismounted.

"Yes, sir."

Jack gave his mount a pat on the muzzle. "Sorry, Ptolemy, old boy. If I should discover why I am in such a ridiculous hurry, I shall tell you."

"Sir?"

Jack looked to young Thomas. He noted that knowing

expression in Thomas's eyes that he had come to recognize. Timothy and Thomas had been communicating in that strange way again.

"Speak, then."

Thomas held his gaze. "There is a new gentlemun at Ralston. A Yankee."

"Is that all?"

"Yes, Sir."

"Very good. Thank you, Thomas." He turned and set off for the house.

Bloody devil! A Yankee at Ralston! Of course it was the old scoundrel Lionel D'Eauville, who found he could not bear to control his daughter from an ocean away after all! He must have set to sea less than a fortnight after Miss D'Eauville's departure. Even now, he must be gloating over the capture of Lord Johnston, and Miss D'Eauville quite resigned to her decision. Of course, she would never seriously consider an ineligible dolt as himself!

Not that he would be insane enough to marry her!

Lord Weyland exploded into his front hall and was ten full paces toward his study before his butler caught up with him. Jack thrust his lap desk into his servant's arms, followed by riding gloves and hat.

"Sir, would you care to—"

"No, I would not. Place the desk in my study." Jack started down the hall once more.

"Sir, your aunt is asking for you. She is in the afternoon room."

Jack turned on his heel and veered right without breaking stride. The afternoon room door stood open. Jack stepped through.

To his immense relief, the room was empty of all but his aunt. She sat in her favorite wing chair, needlework in her hands.

"Good afternoon, Aunt."

"There you are. I believe it would do me no good to ask where you have been these past two hours."

"I have been experiencing nature." Jack sat in the chair opposite Aunt Bea. "I felt a yen to spend time away from two-legged creatures."

"That is all very well for *you*," Aunt Bea fumed. She continued with her precise embroidery stitches, frowning at the linen in her hands. "I can hardly do the same, can I?"

"You seem to be alone just now."

"I am at the mercy of fate. I know not when I shall be disturbed next by some morose woman or other. Mrs. Millington came downstairs only long enough to complain, and Miss Millington came flying into the house in tears a short while ago." Aunt Bea sniffed, then continued. "Mr. Millington is snoring in the study, but fortunately I could have the door closed to reduce the noise. In any event, John Burke Weyland, I should like to know what you have done to upset Miss Millington today."

Jack knew he was in deep trouble with his aunt. He had not heard his full name on her lips in a very long time, and it always boded ill.

Jack cleared his throat. "Not a thing. I did not even see her this afternoon."

"Oh, I see. She took a walk and saw a sight so very distressing that it sent her home in hysterics." Aunt Bea said this in a tone that indicated she did not believe this at all. But a thought occurred to Jack.

He knew what Miss Millington might have seen. Perhaps she had seen Miss D'Eauville and himself! The place was near enough for it to be possible. Good Lord.

"But then," Aunt Bea went on, "she sees so very little of you. That might very well be the trouble. While you are in the thrall of the lovely Miss D'Eauville, Miss Millington might not exist."

Jack slapped his chair arm in exasperation. "Aunt, I love you, but you must know that I am *not* in Miss D'Eauville's thrall, nor anyone else's. I am but taking appropriate time to consider a thing as important as matrimony. Also, you may as well know, Miss D'Eauville has accepted Lord Johnston's proposal of marriage. She has told me herself."

"Do not raise your voice to me, young sir!" Aunt Bea thrust her needlework onto the occasional table beside her. "I am telling you what I see—what I am going through. Now my point has been proven! Miss D'Eauville is a headstrong, thoughtless, selfish being, just as her father was! She has trampled your heart and in so doing, Miss Millington's—not to mention mine! I shall never see a—a child before I die—" Aunt Bea's voice choked off, and she retrieved her handkerchief from her bodice.

"Aunt Bea, do not distress yourself—" Jack came to his feet.

Aunt Bea dabbed at the corner of her eye with the handkerchief, but she held Jack's gaze fiercely. "I did not have a child of my own. You are all I have. I will hold no infant in my arms if I cannot hold yours!"

"Aunt . . ."

She covered her eyes with her handkerchief, and Jack stood helplessly watching her. He had never seen his aunt weep . . . not since his mother had died.

"Aunt, let me get you tea."

"I do not want tea," came her husky voice.

Jack walked slowly to his aunt's side, hesitated a moment, then lay a hand on her shoulder.

"What has Miss D'Eauville's father to do with this?"

Bea drew breath. "Nothing at all. Only that he did as he pleased, just as his daughter is doing—and just as *you* are doing—while I molder here like a fool!"

"I shall marry," he said quietly.

She shook her head. "No. You are quite right. You must not unless it is your own wish."

"You wished to be married," he said, "but for me, you are not."

"That is not true. For my sister, and then for your father, I was not."

"And for my sister and me."

Aunt Bea sniffed into her handkerchief, then stoically dabbed her eyes and looked up. "No. I might have married. But I chose to stay here."

"Aunt, you never told this to me."

"To what end should I have told you? It is in the past."

"I am sorry, Aunt. I wish your choices had been happier."

Jack squeezed her shoulder gently, and his aunt reached up and covered his hand with hers.

"I *did* make a happy choice, Jack. And now, I must not make yours."

Jack sought the right response, something understanding, something that conveyed the love in his heart. But just then, a summons came from the doorway. Jack looked to see his butler with a note on a silver salver.

Jack left his aunt's side and took up the missive. "That is all, Bates."

"What is it?" asked Aunt Bea.

The butler departed, and Jack quickly unfolded the vellum. Matters, it seemed, were moving quickly.

"It is an invitation to dinner at Ralston. Lionel D'Eauville has arrived."

Jack looked to his aunt, and saw that her face had gone white.

Chapter Fourteen

*L*ionel D'Eauville arrived at Ralston his big, boom-
ing, flamboyant self. He was full of tales of his
adventures and his current state of fortune, repeatedly
expressed his delight in being "home" again, and
claimed all was as he had left it.

Charles, who believed he had accomplished much in
the way of improvement since his grandfather's time,
kept his annoyance to himself, and greeted his American uncle with warmth and enthusiasm. The anticipated
infusion of much-needed funds from his uncle did
much to better his mood. Indeed, Lionel D'Eauville accepted the news of his daughter's choice of Lord Johnston with such wholeheartedness that Charles saw his
financial rescue as assured.

Cat first saw her father in the library with Charles
and Lord Johnston, and their smiles and mutually con-
gratulatory mood told her that her father had already
approved her match with Lord Johnston. All the men
rose, and Lionel opened his arms. "There she is—my
beautiful daughter! Come and give your father a kiss!"

In a thrice Cat thrust her dismals away, for the sight
of her father, well and hearty, left room for nothing
else. She flew enthusiastically into his embrace and
laughed as his hug took her off her feet.

"My little girl, all grown!"

"My big father, still a gentleman carpenter!"

He landed her once again on her feet, and she gazed up into his handsome, grinning, well-loved face.

"I do believe you missed me, Father!"

"Only a bit. Only the tiniest bit!"

"Did you think I could not manage on my own?"

"Not at all! I knew you would conquer all in less than a twinkling! Therefore, I made haste to come. I must toast you, my dear—I have just had the pleasure of making your Lord Johnston's acquaintance."

"And I," said Lord Johnston, "have had the extreme pleasure of making *yours*, sir. Again, I must compliment your exquisite daughter."

Cat looked at Lord Johnston then. At his side, her cousin Charles beamed; but while Lord Johnston smiled, Cat noted that his eyes did not. If she had had any fancy once that Lord Johnston might truly have a preference for her, that idea was now put to rest.

She had not set out to win hearts . . . but now it seemed to matter.

"Father, I would love for us to take a walk, and you can tell me all about Ralston," she said, still smiling. "Just the two of us, and we will have a good talk. Shall we?"

Her father gave her a wink. "My dear, I have only just arrived. I must be a good guest and visit with your cousin and fiancé. And I have yet to see our Rebecca, whom I hear has done famously as well." He laid his hands upon her shoulders then, and gazed lovingly down at her. "You have made me very, very happy, Catherine. I have been hoping for just such a son-in-law as Lord Johnston."

Cat's heart sank. Matters appeared to be very bleak, indeed. But she must, she simply *must*, think of a way to resolve her dilemma without breaking her father's heart.

A few hours later the reply to the night's dinner invitation arrived from Weyland. The invitation was regretfully declined, explaining that Miss Southrop did not feel quite well and all decided to stay home. Cat received this missive for examination from Susan, and with it in hand, Cat at last drew Becky aside for a consultation.

The two ladies strolled through the garden at Ralston, certain of privacy, as the gentlemen had gone off shooting. Still, Cat continued down the flagstone path until the yew hedge hid them from view before speaking.

"Becky, I am in need of your sound advice. I have received some most surprising information. I confess I am at a complete loss."

Becky glanced at her. "What can this be? I never knew you not to know exactly what to do."

"Yes. It is absurd, is it not? But nevertheless, here I am. It seems that Father agreed to pay a substantial sum of money to Charles when I make a match of which Father approves. And Charles is deep in debt."

Becky raised her brows. "How inconsiderate of him."

"Oh, it was not Charles's fault. His father had already run through most of the money before Charles inherited."

"Goose. I meant it is thoughtless of your father to make such an agreement. He most certainly knew that you could be trusted to make the best decision. I wonder that you did not tell me of it before."

"I did not because I did not know. Lord Weyland, however, did know. He told me this very afternoon."

"Did he, though?" Becky sounded appropriately incensed. "It does seem as though the gentlemen have imagined they have had the whole of the business in hand. I am surprised about Lord Weyland, however. I had thought he was a bit . . . encouraging of your attention, as much as you would not have him."

In a rush Cat recalled the feeling of Lord Weyland's arms around her. The memory had the power of warming her still. He was not on her list, and he had declared in his journal that she frightened him as much as she intrigued him. That two such people could desire each other so was a puzzlement indeed.

She sighed. "I can forgive them all for disappointing *me*. But I cannot have what I want without making everyone else unhappy, which I cannot allow. And I do *not* wish to marry Lord Johnston."

Becky looked at her, and Cat met her gaze. Becky smiled. "I thought you would never realize it."

"I do not wonder. I know I seem impossibly selfish. I cannot fear a reputation of putting others before myself."

"Oh, hush, Cat. I always knew that you are not selfish at all. It is for that very reason that I feared you would make a choice with only your father's happiness in mind. I was afraid, my dear, that you would never realize how to make yourself happy as well."

"Whether I realize it or not, my choices are the same. Father would not approve of Lord Weyland."

Becky halted on the path, bringing Cat to a stop beside her. "Is this true?"

"Of course it is true. I would not tell you if it were not true. You know very well that my father aspires to an earl for me at the very least."

"No, foolish dear! Is it true that you want to marry Lord Weyland?"

"Yes."

The two female cousins stared at each other.

"Oh, my dear Cat. You *do* realize . . ." Becky stepped up to Cat and embraced her, and Cat returned her cousin's affectionate hug.

"I should like to know," Becky said at last, "how Lord Weyland knew of your father's agreement with Charles. *You* may forgive him, but I insist on being very put out by him."

"He and Charles are lifelong friends. After thinking it over, I know that he cannot be fairly blamed. So there you have it . . . if I could act in a completely selfish manner, Lord Weyland would not comply. He has already declined to marry me."

"Oh, I see."

The two ladies began to walk again.

"And now Lord Weyland will not come to dinner tonight," said Cat.

"I am not surprised, given all you have said."

"Nor am I. When I spoke to Lord Weyland this afternoon . . . things went rather badly." Cat hesitated. "Oh, Becky. It is shocking, but I have been such a hen brain! I was so convinced that I knew what would make me happy! But it was not until I saw you in love . . . Oh, bother. Do not listen to me, Becky."

"You cannot say anything that will hurt me. I know you too well."

"I am impossible—Nanny Jane always said so."

"And she loves you to death."

The two ladies resumed walking.

"Have you spoken with your father?" Becky asked.

"No, not as yet. I shall try. But I am certain that Father's mind is fixed on the subject of my marriage. He has talked of it forever. He so enjoyed our list-making."

Becky sighed. "Of all the times for me to be without anything wise to say. I shall think on it." She paused. "May I see the note?"

Wordlessly Cat gave it to her, and they continued walking while Becky read. The cool of the apple grove wrapped around them, and they stepped through puddles of dappled shade and sunlight.

At last Becky refolded the missive. "I hope Lord Weyland's aunt is not truly ill."

Cat sighed. "I do not believe Lord Weyland is the sort of gentleman who would tell an untruth about his aunt on his own account. She must in fact be unable to come."

As suddenly as that, inspiration struck her like a lightening bolt. Cat felt blood rushing through her veins again, the familiar surge of confidence and anticipation. She lifted her head and looked at Becky. "I wonder . . . it seems that Miss Southrop knew my father at one time. How my wits have gone begging! Perhaps . . . yes, perhaps . . . she is not ill at all!"

"Miss D'Eauville," announced Bates somberly. Before a breath could be drawn by either lady in Beatrice Southrop's good morning parlor, Miss Catherine D'Eauville swept past the butler, rosy cheeked, eyes aglow, the purple plume in her plum velvet hat switching madly with her every step.

Bea suppressed her own appearance of surprise, she hoped, but she was certain Miss D'Eauville had observed Mrs. Millington's look of astonishment, particularly as that look dissolved into cold annoyance.

The chill, however, seemed to be felt by everyone but Miss D'Eauville. Bea was struck with the thought that if a wild beast were to leap into the room, the exuberant and flamboyant Miss Cat would not notice it, either.

"Good morning, ladies!" Cat exclaimed. "Such a marvelous morning! I had to take out my cousin's mare so I might feel the lovely breeze and the sun. You so rarely seem to have sun here! But how I do go on. Miss Southrop, I was so concerned about news of your health I was simply *required* to call as soon as I possibly could. So here you see me, and my father just come from America!"

Bea sat frozen in a kind of trance. Miss Catherine took herself to the wing chair near Bea and seated herself, her smile unabated at the lack of invitation. Of course, Bea would have invited her, but the girl simply moved before Bea could think to do it. Merciful heavens, what did she do now?

"Good morning, Miss D'Eauville," Bea said. "Will you have tea?"

"Are you quite well, then?" Miss Catherine cocked her head and looked charming. Indeed, in her striking hat, violet gown, and plum velvet spencer with gold frog closures, she appeared stunningly beautiful in her grand, demonstrative way. Miss Catherine did, indeed, remind Bea of Mr. Lionel.

Bea's heart skipped. Mr. Lionel—it seemed impossible that Mr. Lionel could be at Ralston again.

"I *do* hope you are well," Miss Catherine continued. "My father, in particular, desired to know."

Bea looked once more at Lionel's daughter, and was caught in the gaze of her lively brown eyes. Had Lionel in truth thought of her? From somewhere she found the strength to draw her next breath.

"I am recovered, as you see."

"I am so glad." Miss Catherine immediately turned her attention to Mrs. Millington, who had heretofore sat quietly with a disapproving look on her face, pursuing her needlework.

"You must have heard the news of my engagement to Lord Johnston," Miss Catherine said cheerfully. "My father is so pleased. He does not care that I do not marry a fortune, for as he says, 'I have that. I simply want my only daughter to marry a good English title.' I, on the other hand, do not think so very much about titles, for I am an American, after all. But Lord Johnston is a very agreeable gentleman, I shall grant that."

What, Bea thought, possessed Miss Catherine's wits? She seemed completely oblivious to the fact that Mrs. Millington was very disinclined toward her. Mr. Lionel's daughter was not so like him after all, for Mr. Lionel had always been extremely penetrating when it served him to be so. Bea thought frantically for a way to intervene. Alas, with Miss Catherine inheriting her father's headstrong qualities, Bea could not readily determine a way to stop her.

"Of course Lord Johnston is an agreeable gentleman," Mrs. Millington snapped. "He is *English*."

Now the cat is in the broth, thought Bea.

Cat raised her dark brows ever so little. Her smile

grew. "Yes—and he is an earl. How very fortunate I must find myself to be. I need an earl to marry me, and Lord Johnston is compelled to take a rich but common wife. Oh, and this puts me in mind of something. Are *you* not searching for a match for *your* daughter, Mrs. Millington?"

Mrs. Millington's complexion darkened another shade.

"My daughter is presently walking in the garden with *Lord Weyland*," she said frostily.

"Oh," Miss Catherine said. "I am *so* sorry. And here I am boasting of my engagement with an earl!"

Bea snatched in a breath. "I think I shall call for cakes."

That was but a ridiculous punctuation of the moment. Mrs. Millington rose majestically to her feet.

"I—shan't—have—cake," she pronounced icily. "I have a headache. Excuse me." She turned and stalked out the morning room door.

Miss Catherine gazed after her a moment, a thoughtful—or was it a calculating?—look on her face. Then she turned to Bea.

"Oh, dear. I think I have said something wrong."

Good Lord, Bea thought. Miss Catherine did not look calculating at all. She looked . . . *pleased*. Lionel's daughter was about something, and Bea was afraid to learn what it was. However, she knew that nothing good would come from any attempt to avoid the inevitable.

"Miss D'Eauville," Bea said sternly, "what is your purpose? Do not say you are merely here to wish me well."

Miss Catherine's eyes widened, sparkling in sudden intensity, and she leaned forward in her chair and pointed a long, gloved finger at Bea.

"Oh, how excellent of you! I do so love a frank talk. A conversation is so much more stimulating, do you not think, when it is between equals in intellect and daring? Very well, I shall tell you why I have come."

She paused just long enough to draw breath. "I have come to make Mrs. Millington as jealous as I possibly can of my wonderful match, and to put everyone on their ears. Is it not quite dreadful of me? Only think, even now Mrs. Millington is wishing for an earl for her daughter above all else, even an earl with a fortune made up of naught but hopes!"

Bea gasped. "Miss D'Eauville, I cannot believe my ears!"

"Oh, but you shall. You see, I am not so bad as all that. I truly wish to interest the Millingtons in my fiancé. I do believe that Lord Johnston and Miss Millington would make the most excellent marriage."

"Miss D'Eauville! Do you not realize that the Millingtons have *intentions* for their daughter and my nephew?"

"Oh, quite. But does your nephew love Miss Millington?"

"I—I—But that is neither here nor there! You are engaged to Lord Johnston!"

Miss D'Eauville sighed. "Oh, but do you not think that a modern marriage must be a match of love? I admit, I have been of a different mind myself, but I have come to know a little more about it."

"Love!" Bea's indignance swelled. "What can you know about love? It is the most absurd thing to use in choosing a future spouse. Marriage is far too important an issue. No civilized marriage is based on love!"

Miss Catherine's smile returned, but it was a softer smile, a knowing smile.

"Were you once in love with my father, Miss Southrop?"

This time it took Bea only the time of a blink to realize that if anyone could be so bold, it was Lionel's daughter. Her heart made a jarring leap—a bad thing, she thought, for a woman of her age—particularly as it had recently jarred just so when she received the news that Mr. Lionel had arrived in England.

"Miss D'Eauville, is there ever a thing in your head that you will not say?"

Cat laughed lightly. "I think there must be. My father brought me up to be very discreet, you see."

"Discreet!" Bea exclaimed. "Oh, my *word*." She broke off, lay her needlework aside, and turned a direct gaze back upon Miss Cat. It took all the strength she could summon. "Mr. Lionel and yourself, discreet! I *never*. I do think, however, that he has taught you his sense of the absurd."

"So you *did* know him very well," Cat said.

Bea let out her breath in a huff. "I have admitted to an acquaintance with him. But that is far and wide from being in love with him, which I assure you, Miss D'Eauville, I should never confide to you even if it were true. Why do you not take all such 'discreet' questions to your father?"

"I cannot. It would be so indelicate to ask him of a lady he knew before he married my mother! But *you* can have no scruple against breaking my heart." Cat smiled again, somewhat whimsically. "I hope you know that I jest. I shall not suffer to hear the truth. I do not remember my mother at all. She is but a pretty woman in a portrait, and father scarcely ever spoke of her."

Bea picked up her needlework once more, hoping that Cat could not see how her fingers trembled.

"I am very sorry for that. I wish I could help you, but your father never spoke to me of her, either. I believe the sum of my information was contained in the line, 'by the time you read this missive, I shall be married to Miss Amelia Prescott.' And *that* was contained in a letter to your grandfather, not to myself."

Cat hesitated for only a moment. "Of course, he has never married again."

"Then one might conclude that he is happy as he is."

"Oh, Father has never been happy as he is. He is forever thinking of something that seems impossible to have, then determining how to get it, I think. Some of those things he could not have for himself, however. That is why I am to become a Countess Someone-or-Other. But somehow I fear that this will not make him happy, either."

"Oh?" Bea looked up. Her heart gave a warning flutter.

Miss Catherine tipped her head inquisitively to one side. Too late.

"Why did you not marry my father?"

Bea opened her mouth then closed it again. There! The thud came again. Then her heart continued to beat, telling her that there was to be no merciful escape from Lionel's daughter.

She tossed her needlework aside and turned a militant face upon her interrogator. "Might you tell me why the answers to all your impertinent questions are so very important to you?"

Miss Catherine blinked. Her brown eyes were suddenly soft. "Because I want to marry your nephew, Miss Southrop, and I hoped that you could help. You see, I am in love with him."

Chapter Fifteen

With the news of Miss D'Eauville's betrothal, the mood of the gathering at Ralston Hall changed. The contest was over, and it was time for celebration. Even Lord Macclesby stayed and effected a happy face; Charles felt grimly that Macclesby stayed to eat and drink at Charles's expense. But the guests were soon removed from Charles's responsibility. Mr. D'Eauville proclaimed that any celebration of his daughter's future establishment was to be funded from his own pocket, and consequently directed that as many invitations as possible be extended to the events at Ralston Hall.

Mr. D'Eauville savored his victory, the culmination of years of hope. Those who had never known Mr. Lionel quickly knew him for Miss D'Eauville's father—incredibly, he overshadowed even his daughter's exuberant personality. Mr. D'Eauville told tales of his adventures and indulged the guests with his rapier wit and sometimes overwhelming bonhomie. In addition, he ordered kegs of ale and an enormous quantity of food for a feast to be set before the tenants; and in no time at all he was known as an outstanding gentleman, sprung from the true seed of his noble ancestors, and well deserving of whatever good fate came his way.

Two days passed without the promised ride with his daughter while Mr. Lionel D'Eauville continued to

warm himself in his moment of triumph. It was not that
Lionel was an uncaring father; he loved his daughter
with all his heart, but he saw her perfectly engaged
with enjoying herself. Also, he was certain he knew his
daughter, and he knew she rejoiced with him. Had she
not always wanted what he wanted?

Twenty-four years ago he had sailed from England
with nothing in his pocket save hope. He had returned
at age forty-seven a wealthy man, his daughter engaged
to marry an earl. And the home of his childhood . . .
he gazed about himself and found it hard to believe
that now, the means to save it was in his hands. His
nephew was mortgaged to the hilt and at a stand without his help.

Cat continued laughing and joking with her usual
exuberance, her demeanor showing nothing to suggest
anything was amiss with her. But on the third morning
that dawned, Mr. D'Eauville found his daughter waiting for him in the breakfast room.

"Good morning, Father," she said cheerfully, rising
to kiss him on the cheek. "Shall I pour your tea?"

"Ah, how I long for a good ale! But tea shall do. I
must remember who I am, after all."

Lionel seated himself at last next to his beautiful
daughter at the breakfast table, his plate mounded with
a laborer's portion of cold meats. There was no one else
in the room; Lionel credited that to lazy habits in general, even though he had met with others on the previous two mornings at this time. Then he dismissed the
thought.

"Have some of this preserve, Father. Lady D'Eauville
says it is from an old receipt your mother used to like.
Shall I spread it for you?"

Lionel gazed down into his daughter's guileless face.

"Cat, I detest preserves, and furthermore, you know
this very well! What are you about?"

"Why, nothing, Father. It is just that it has been so

long since I have seen you." Cat demurely picked up her thin slice of bread and began spreading it with the preserve.

"Tell me what it is. I may as well know now."

She looked at him and smiled. "Well, there is one small matter."

"As I thought."

"We have not spoken as father and daughter should about matters at hand, and you have been here three days."

"Go on!" he said, staring. "You think that way, do you?"

"Yes. And I would like us to have a private coze today, dear Father, before I am forced to take severe measures." She took a bite of her bread and gazed at him, chewing, a twinkle in her eyes.

He sighed. "Very well."

"Ride with me. I would not like to be interrupted with this one or that one of your flatterers."

"Or of your own, I'd bet."

It was an unusually beautiful morning when they set out. Father and daughter being much similar, they set their horses to run as soon as practical. They slowed at the top of the distant hill that overlooked Ralston, and both drew up their mounts to gaze at the panorama around them.

Cat drew a deep breath of damp, fresh English air. The scene she beheld she now had committed to memory, but it still captured her with its beauty. The rolling green of the fields, the patchwork of hedges, the sentinel phalanx of trees at the forest's edge—all were beauties to behold, even without the noble Ralston Hall resting in the center of the scene, demanding attention of its own.

She turned her head just slightly, and saw that her father was gazing about as well, a brooding frown between his eyes.

"Father! Why so dismal? I had thought you giddy with joy."

"Daughter, you have a way with jest that is unappealing betimes."

"As is your way of evasion, sir. I believe your thoughts are of more than your *victorious* return—" Here, Cat fanned one arm wide, causing her mare to toss her head. "—and your daughter's upcoming nuptials."

"There you are wrong. I cannot be more delighted. Come, my dear, let us ride."

Cat complied without a word, but guided her mare toward the estate of Lord Weyland. Their direction did not go without his notice, however.

"I should as soon ride the opposite way along the wood," he said.

"I should not. There is the most delightful estate this way. You must surely know it. The inhabitant is Lord Weyland, and a very good friend he is to Charles, as well. You have not met him as yet."

"Yes, I know it would be the Weyland estate. It is still in the family, then. Is there a lady of the house?"

"Lord Weyland is not married."

"I did not ask that."

Cat felt her conscience jolt painfully—but there was nothing to do but evade this small issue. She suspected, no, was certain, that if Father knew Miss Southrop was still in residence, he would turn his horse then and there.

"Well, it is *my* conversation, Father. It is *I* who wished to speak to *you*. And it is of Lord Weyland that I wish to speak." She laughed.

"Oh?"

Her father's single word conveyed more than paragraphs.

Cat raised her chin, staring straight ahead between her mare's ears. "He is a most extraordinary gentleman. He is clever beyond all things. You shall see. He is just the sort you like."

Her father grunted. "And just why do you wish me to meet this *extraordinary* gentleman," he said, "when I have already met your future husband, who should command your every thought?"

"How unutterably silly. Lord Johnston does not command my every thought, Father. I shudder to think what I would be if he did."

Father drew his horse to a stop. Cat, ears attentive, quickly came to a halt herself and turned her mare around to face him.

"Catherine Amelia Prescott D'Eauville," he pronounced in a sonorous tone. "Explain yourself."

Cat tilted her head slightly to one side and regarded her father intently. "My fiancé," she said, "has not the sense to wear his hat in the rain."

Her father stared back at her. "No sense? I thought he had sense."

"He has sense enough to wish to marry me, and he is an earl, although I do not believe sense is a qualification for that."

"Are you telling me that you do not wish to marry Johnston?"

"Am I? I am confusing, am I not? No, I am extremely fortunate to meet an earl as senseless as Lord Johnston. I count my blessings daily."

Her father's face relaxed slightly. "Ah, you jest. But you are worried, then, my girl? No need. No need at all. A big, strong, nimble-witted girl like you will have no difficulty. Even a *senseless* man like Johnston will know how to deal with marriage, never fear. Damn, I wish Mrs. Mac-Caluff were here. I should have thought—"

"Oh, no, I do not need Nanny Jane. I simply wish you to meet Lord Weyland. And do not tell me I should be thinking of Johnston. For all that he is a nice man, I spend more than enough time with him. We are not in love, after all."

Her father's frown returned. "This is a fine time to think of that."

"Of course it is. I would not want to be thinking of it after our wedding. He is an earl, and that is what we wanted. He should not restrict my freedom, and that is what *I* wanted."

"Well." He paused, perusing her face. "You shall come to like him better." His frown suddenly vanished, as if a wind had blown his doubts from his mind. "And now, I am sending you down to London, my dear, to get a wardrobe that would set the ladies of Boston fainting in envy. What do you think of that?"

Cat stared back in dismay. She could not have this. All of her plans would be overturned. She *must* stay at Ralston. A fortnight—even a week—would make all the difference in the happiness of so many.

"You like your gowns," he said. "And your hats—I never saw you visit a town unless you bought at least a half dozen hats." He paused. Then Cat detected almost a plea in his eyes, carefully veiled, but she knew her beloved father very well.

Cat sighed. She must give Father some acceptable answer, else he would demand to know all. "Oh, Father. Very well . . . I shall go to London. But only on the condition that you meet Lord Weyland first."

"Lord Almightly. Send him an invitation."

"No, I want you to meet him today. We only have to ride just a little distance more. Please, Father."

Lionel hesitated, but the expression on his daughter's face determined his answer. "Very well, little girl. Lead the way, since you seem to know it."

Weyland was again alone with nagging thoughts. He resented it, as they distracted him from his important business from time to time. He did dutifully record them in his log, along with his collected observations of Miss D'Eauville and associates, for that was of course important to his studies. But he could not distance himself as he liked.

The devil had been in that kiss.

He thought about it as he inspected his beehives on an afternoon several days after the arrival of Mr. Lionel D'Eauville. The process involved the beekeeper standing by operating the smoke pot as Jack looked at the combs, one by one, in his movable frame hive—a much easier process than with the plain box hive his father had used.

The task of inspecting still required Jack's careful attention, but left enough of his mind free to ponder other concerns. By nature, once presented with a problem, Jack pursued it in an objective, scientific manner, and as he was forced to categorize the matter of Miss D'Eauville as a problem, he turned possible actions over in his mind.

Jack had taken a modest inheritance and increased it by wise management, including application of modern agricultural practices, careful expenditure and investment, and a system of providing financial reward to his farmers. He was proud of what he had done with the family fortune, and properly so. It made him sufficiently comfortable to enable him to make a respectable gift to Charles, if need be, to keep his friend from complete ruin should Miss D'Eauville's father withdraw his offer of monetary reward.

That Charles would not accept it was a strong possibility, however, and Jack could not think his way around that obstacle.

"She be looking clean, sir?" asked Rob, the beekeeper.

"Very much so. Let us go to the next."

The other damnable problem was Miss D'Eauville's happiness. Jack could not think she could be happy if her father was crushed by disappointment. Then there was the matter of the tricky situation with Miss Millington.

When examined from all directions, there seemed no possibility of his marriage with Miss D'Eauville.

There! Yes, it was true. He wanted to marry her. Now, if only he could find reasons for *that*!

"I fears we lost th' queen in this one, sir."

"Hm."

Surprisingly, now he *could* find reasons for marrying her. She was happy, healthy, strong, and intelligent. She would have happy, healthy, strong, and intelligent children. It was simply not a matter that a scientific gentleman could deny. And blessedly, the getting of children from her would be pleasure beyond comprehension. Of course he could justify marrying her now that it was impossible!

His ruminations, and his inspection, were interrupted by a piercing screech.

"Ei-eeeeee!"

Jack turned swiftly. There, from the orchard some twenty paces away, raced a frightened young woman, skirts and apron clutched in one hand, her other hand flailing frantically around her mobcapped head. Behind her lumbered a stout groom, who appeared to be making no increase on the swift-footed maid. He bellowed after her. "Lola! Hold up! Lola—!"

" 'Er is 'eaded this way, sir," said the beekeeper.

"Bees," muttered Jack.

"I 'spect so."

As he watched, the girl veered and started up the side lawn toward the front of the house.

"Put the hive right, Rob." Jack started after the girl at a dead run.

"There it is, Father! Is it not the sweetest place in all of England?"

They had just drawn their horses to a halt at the top of the rise. Lionel looked at his daughter, transfixed on the panorama before her, then gazed back at the Weyland estate. It was picturesque, he supposed, although it lacked the size and considerable grandeur of Ralston Hall. But at his daughter's fascination, he was forced to view the old home of Miss Beatrice Southrop with new eyes.

It was dignified in its ancient way, neat, and stately. It dominated the next rise on which it stood, beyond and somewhat below them, and was very prettily set off by the orchards behind it, the forest and hills beyond, and the very well-maintained stables to its south. It looked comfortable and content, for all its old stone walls . . . and it made his stomach knot up in such a way as he had not felt for a quarter of a century.

He was not sure if either his daughter or he were actually seeing, but only feeling.

". . . and he has a telescope, Father, for viewing the heavens. It is there in the upper left-hand tower. And books! His library is full of books about all kinds of things. I should dearly love a chance to browse them."

He was forced to bring his attention to his daughter's words.

"I think I should perhaps feel relieved that you have not yet had the chance, except I am wondering how you happened to view the telescope. That is not the drawing room that you indicated it is in."

His daughter's cheeks were tinged slightly pink, but they did not seem to change at his comment. "He showed me, Father. Do not worry! You know me better than to suspect me of foolishness!" She glanced at him, smiling, then looked quickly back at the manor. He eyes had been very, very bright.

She had feelings for this Weyland. He had hoped not, but there it was. Weyland, he knew, was no more than a baron.

"I know you well enough to suspect you of impulsiveness," he said. His horse shifted restlessly beneath him. "But there, we may as well go on and see this paragon you speak of."

He urged his horse forward, and Cat followed suit. They rode down the hill together, and up the next grade at a slow trot. Lionel inhaled the smell of it, the rich earth, the early summer blooms—nothing unusual, he told himself, and yet it seemed to belong uniquely to this place and his memories. At the next juncture, they were riding across the parkland approach, and the manor grew in size. Cat, he saw, had a smile on her face that seemed permanently affixed, and the old sensation assailed him again. His memory jarred, and a slender, golden-haired girl stood staring up at him. The blue bow in her hair had loosened, and the freed locks blew gently about her lovely, earnest face.

> *"If only my sister were not so ill."*
> *"If only I had a fortune."*
> *"I wish none of it mattered."*
> *"It does, my sweet. It does."*

Lionel blinked. Damn. Bea was gone and grown old, he was older still, and there was nothing worth thinking of now. She belonged to his past, to a road not chosen.

The house was near. They approached from the northeasterly direction, with a full view of the east side of the manor and the trees behind it.

At that moment, a high-pitched scream reached his ears. Instantly he and Cat stopped their horses abreast of each other.

Before their wondering eyes, the figure of a young woman burst from the trees, running for all she was worth. A man followed, jogging ponderously, calling after her. But the maid ran as if death was at her heels, and the stout young man was considerably slower than either death or the maid. Her mobcap flew off. The wind took it, and it fluttered up like a wounded dove.

Then, from around the back corner of the house, a long-legged gentleman came racing, wearing an odd flat hat with a strange veil flying behind him. He made rapid advance after the terrified girl, and near the front corner of the house, he caught her by one arm, jerked off his neckcloth and began frantically flailing the air around them. The girl shrieked and screamed the more, fighting him madly and slapping at the air around her head like a maddened thing. The gentleman flung the neckcloth, swept the girl up in his arms, and raced with her around the near corner of the house toward the front.

In the midst of this, a gigantic mongrel dog came bounding across the yard from the direction of the stable, barking ferociously. The gentleman hurdled up the stately front steps, kicked the great door, and as it came open, leapt inside. The girl's shrieks faded, echoing hollowly off polished wood and tile, and the door slammed shut behind them—much to the disappointment of the dog, who bounded up the steps only to be met with defeat.

Lionel looked at his daughter. Cat, he saw, was already regarding him with a tentative expression.

"Was that your paragon?" he asked.

She blinked. "Indeed, Father, I believe it was."

Chapter Sixteen

"No, daughter, I rather believe I should like to visit your Extraordinary Gentleman now, after all. It promises interesting developments."

Her father set course determinedly toward Weyland Hall, and Cat had no choice but to follow, turning ideas over in her head as quickly as she could seize upon them. The time did not seem in the *least* advantageous for a call on Lord Weyland. Cat also knew that her father would not be deterred. He had caught nose of a fox; and besides, the outrageous scene they had just witnessed augured well for the kind of entertainment he dearly loved.

As they gained the lawn proper, the maid's stout young man lumbered around the front corner of the house, his course set for the front entrance where the supposed object of his affections had vanished. Yet another person appeared from the area of the back garden, an elderly workman, plodding phlegmatically after the rest, a dour look about him.

"Perhaps you should stay back," Mr. D'Eauville said cheerily. "I believe we may have fisticuffs."

"Nonsense, Father. It is all perfectly innocent. I am quite sure there is a very sound reason for what we saw."

"I cannot think what it could be," Cat's father replied, "unless the young woman were on fire."

"Father, I am coming with you. I rather think that *you* shall need protection from *me*."

Her father raised his brows, giving her a droll look. "Hm. Might you be acquainted with that great maleficent hound?" He turned his gaze on the wolfish animal, who sat mournfully staring up at the closed door.

"I am."

Her father glanced back at her, eyes twinkling. "Well, then—you may go first."

Cat laughed.

As if by magic, Lord Weyland's Timothy-Thomas appeared in the front lawn to meet them. They finished their ride across the lawn, and Cat flashed a quick smile at the twin as her father assisted her to dismount.

The young man had passed the dog-guardian and entered, as had the old workman, both apparently knowing the beast. But as Cat and her father approached the steps, Boofus turned and stared at them. A deep rumble came from his throat.

But it was only for the briefest moment. Cat stepped forward and held her hand out enticingly. "Come, you good boy. Come, Boofus."

The dog's features transformed into a look of elation. He bounced down the steps, and Cat, barely avoiding being tumbled over by his affection, scratched him thoroughly behind his ears.

"Boofus, is it?" her father asked.

Cat ignored him. "Boofus, stay. There's a good boy."

At last Cat convinced Boofus to stand with all fours on the ground, and she then preceded her father up the front steps. He knocked vigorously, and received no answer.

"Extraordinary circumstances call for extraordinary measures," he said with assurance. He opened the door and stepped inside.

Cat followed. They found themselves alone in the front hall, but the sound of voices, punctuated by loud sobbing, led them to the open doors to the back parlor.

Cat recognized it as the morning room where Lord Weyland had taken her to visit with Miss Southrop.

Lord Weyland's calming tones floated out into the hall. ". . . She is quite well, Michael. She is frightened, that is all."

"Them things was a'ter her som'thin' fierce, they was!"

"Yes, and so I observed. They were attracted by something about her. Lola—Lola, please calm yourself."

Cat and her father arrived in the doorway. Lord Weyland stood by the sofa, upon which lay a white-faced girl, who was attempting to muffle her sobs in a handkerchief. Beside Lord Weyland was another maid, her back turned to the door, leaning solicitously over the girl. Standing back farther, between the doorway and the sofa, clearly winded and distraught, stood the stout young man, twisting his cap in his hands. Beside him was the roughly dressed old man, solemn-faced and motionless.

"Are you perhaps wearing scent?" Lord Weyland asked the girl. "I seem to smell something—suggestive of violet."

The girl offered no response but more sobs.

"I—I gave her some," the young man said. "It 'twer my fault!"

"Do not trouble yourself. She suffered only a sting or two, and seems otherwise none the worse. Where is the lemonade?"

Lord Weyland turned toward the doorway—and froze in place. He saw them.

"How do you do?" Cat smiled and stepped forward. "It is bees, I suppose?" She extended her hand, but when Lord Weyland seemed late in gathering his wits, she paused and withdrew her hand. Near her the stout young man stood goggle-eyed, staring at her as well, and from behind she felt her father's keen gaze.

At that moment, the attending maid straightened and

turned. The maid was no maid at all. She was Miss Southrop.

Cat could not see her father's expression, but she clearly saw Miss Southrop's. Bea's eyes widened, her lips parted, and then her face went as pale as the girl's on the sofa. She clutched the damp cloth with which she had been ministering to the girl, her knuckles gone quite white—and she stood, Cat thought, as though her feet had become fastened to the floor.

The girl, miraculously, stopped sobbing, and stared with the rest.

Cat licked her lips. "I am afraid our visit may be slightly inopportune, but my father was quite anxious to visit. Lord Weyland, my father, Mr. D'Eauville. Miss Southrop . . . my father."

"Further introduction is unnecessary, my dear. Miss Southrop and I are acquainted." Cat's father stepped up beside her, and she sensed an unfamiliar tension emanating from his substantial form. She glanced up at her father's profile, and saw he neither smiled nor frowned; there was a curious veil over his usually open expression. She looked back again at Miss Southrop and Lord Weyland.

Lord Weyland seemed suddenly to shake off his momentary paralysis. "I beg your forgiveness," he said. "I was inspecting my beehives, and the young woman passed nearby, wearing scent." He paused, blinked, and lifted his hand to his head and felt the brim of his curious hat. "Forgive me," he said again, and removed the hat. "I keep bees, you see."

Cat gazed at them—at the distraught Miss Southrop in her plain round gown and apron, at a stunned Lord Weyland in his shabby woolen coat and trousers—and dangling the comical hat. It was suddenly too much for Cat. She laughed.

"But you cut such a heroic figure, racing to the young lady's rescue!" Cat gasped for breath. "I had told Father how very extraordinary you are, and you have proved me right!"

Cat had the pleasure of seeing color begin to reappear in the faces of both aunt and nephew.

"It is hardly so amusing as that," Miss Southrop said. Her voice quavered, but she seemed determined. "The poor girl is frightened to death!"

"We are concerned for her well-being, of course," said Lord Weyland. "My bees are very gentle, in the ordinary way."

Cat's father spoke. "Indeed."

Silence.

Cat looked at her father once more. His expression was still blank. But she noticed that his eyes were only for the slender, upright form of Miss Southrop, who stood rigidly before them, her blond tendrils escaping from beneath her cap and wisping about her pretty face. Her gaze, as well, was for his eyes alone, almost as if she were challenging him—or unable to look elsewhere. A storm was arising between them—Cat felt it, much as she sensed the storms blowing in over the ocean at home.

A scratching sound came from behind them. "Sir?" The butler stepped into the room and bowed. Cat and her father moved aside, and some of the tension eased.

Lord Weyland drew breath. "Bates, would you please have Lola assisted to her room to rest, and send her a glass of lemonade. Michael, you may assist."

"Very well, sir," replied Bates. "Would you like any refreshment?"

Miss Southrop intervened. "Yes." Her voice again betrayed the slightest quiver, but it was stronger now. "Tea, please."

"Thank you," Cat's father said, "but it seems we are imposing."

Miss Southrop drew a quick breath. "Nonsense. No one visits my home without taking tea. Bates, bring tea!

Miss D'Eauville and-and Mr. D'Eauville, please do sit
down."

Bates bowed and departed with the stout young man
trailing behind. They were no sooner out the door than
Lord Weyland spoke.

"You may go, John," he said to the old workman.
"We shall finish the hives another day." The old man
touched his cap and left. Then Weyland turned to his
remaining company.

"I must excuse myself. I am not dressed for
company."

"Jack, you are fine as you are!" cried Miss Southrop.
"Everyone knows you have at this moment come in
from inspecting the hives!"

"I shall be back presently, Aunt. I—I really must go."

Lord Weyland started for the door in spite of the
protests of his alarmed aunt.

Cat flashed a smile at her father and Miss Southrop.
"The two of you must have so much to chat about! I
shall excuse myself. Lord Weyland, I wish to see the
bees!" She whirled and hurried after him, ignoring the
calls of both lady and gentleman left behind.

Cat found that Lord Weyland's long strides were
more than a match for hers, even when she abandoned
ladylike form. She was forced to call after him as he
reached the stair.

"Lord Weyland! Wait, please! I must have words
with you!"

He stopped and turned, his face stony, his eyes be-
traying surprise at seeing her darting after him. Lord
Weyland, Cat realized, was more distracted than she
had ever seen him.

"I must see the bees," she said as she came up to
him. She smiled.

He blinked. "Miss D'Eauville, I do not recommend
it. You are wearing scent." His voice was uncharacteristically stiff and aloof.

She laughed lightly. "I am not. And I am not afraid of bees. I will not run. One does not run when visiting bees."

"One young woman did. I should not care to repeat the experience."

Cat huffed. "*Really*, sir. I wish to *speak privately* with you. If you will not visit bees with me, then I shall visit horses with you. Or sheep, or hounds, or baskets of fish! Do you understand me?"

He stared at her face a moment, then a kind of realization dawned in his eyes. She watched as it spread subtly over his face. He sighed.

"Miss D'Eauville," he said wearily, "it will not do. The situation is un-repairable. I have thought about it myself, and I have arrived at no solution. And at this particular time, with—with your unexpected arrival, and with your father—"

Cat hooked her hand under his arm. "Never mind those things," she said soothingly. "Only walk with me. Poor Jack! What a trial you have suffered with me!" She smiled brightly up at him, and saw his features soften.

"Very well. But only for a very short walk. I cannot leave my aunt for any longer than is necessary."

Cat curled her fingers around his hard forearm, which even through the stiff fabric of his coat sent a rivulet of warmth through her. She began conducting him toward the back of the hall, where there was a door into the garden. "Oh, yes, you can," she said. "In fact, you shall *not* return for . . . oh, a half hour, I think."

That he went with her out the door without further protest, Cat counted as one small victory. As they stepped onto the garden path, she said, "So you *do* wish to marry me."

She felt the muscle of his forearm expand slightly beneath her fingers, and knew he had clenched his fist. "I do not think we have—I have spoken to that."

"Of course you have. You have only just told me that you have 'thought about it yourself, and arrived at no solution.' If you have thought about it, sir, then it is something you are in favor of."

He sighed. They walked a little farther along, and Cat inhaled the sweet scent of his late-blooming jonquils. She spied a hawk gliding far up in the sky, circling slowly, watching. Oh, dear heaven, was there hope? In such a beautiful world, on such a glorious day, there must be hope.

"Miss D'Eauville, I am convinced I must surrender and hear what dire scheme you have connived. I shall hear it in due course, and I have learned not to postpone the inevitable."

She exhaled softly. Her heart rose to pound in her temples. "It is simple enough. My father and your aunt were once in love, so we cause them to remember. Then—"

"What are you saying? By what means do you know this?"

"You do not know?" She smiled up at him. "You who know so much apparently do not know love. Not that I will call myself an expert, but it did not take too much time before I could recognize the signs."

"I know only that they were acquainted in her childhood."

"Childhood? How old is your aunt, then? My father left this country at twenty-three years of age, and he is seven and forty now."

Lord Weyland was silent a moment, his quick brain working the figures. She saw when he understood.

"She would not have explained her unhappy love affair to you, I think. Neither would my father have explained it to me. We are left with our cleverness to find it out."

"And if you are wrong? Or, worse still, what if there is nothing but bitterness left between them?"

"I am afraid I must leave all that to them to sort out. I do hope they are not irreconcilable. But I do know my father. He seems all unassailable determination, but he has a soft heart for those he loves."

"If his heart is so soft, then why must you yield to his wishes?"

"Because he is certain that his wishes are best for me, and is afraid to consider any other course. We must show him that we are right." She paused. "We will show him that *his* wishes are not best for *him*."

The path took them around a bend by an oak and followed a towering box hedge. Lord Weyland's pace slowed, and Cat knew he was thinking very hard.

"There is no guarantee that either of them will arrive at the conclusions you have designed for them."

"No. But one must try."

"Your father likely feels ill of me. We must also consider your engagement, and Miss Millington."

"Miss Millington wishes to marry Lord Johnston. And, I rather think, the Millingtons are considering him as well."

At this point, Lord Weyland stopped stock-still, turned, and placed both hands upon her shoulders.

"*What*, if I may ask, have you been doing?"

His gruffness surprised her a little. Cat cocked her head to one side and gazed up at him consideringly. "I hope you have not fallen in love with her after all."

"I want to know what you have done."

"I have observed them, and I have . . . encouraged Mrs. Millington to consider the possibility."

Cat arched her brows and awaited his reply. Her outward appearance must be calm and confident, but—oh, what if she had made a terrible mistake? With all the strength she could muster, she quelled the beginnings of fear—only not that dratted pounding in her throat. She loved this man. Lord Weyland was right for her. He was—he must be.

Lord Weyland's eyelids lowered ever so slightly. Then he released her.

"I see," he said.

"I am sorry if this is a surprise to you. I am, truly. But you see . . . the Millingtons are, after all, more interested in the *status* of one's *sire and dam* than the quality of offspring."

"I am a horse now." Lord Weyland spread his arms. "And a poorly rated horse at that! I am devastated!"

The smile was back in his eyes, and the weight lifted from her heart. She laughed.

"Oh, poor, poor Lord Weyland, rejected by all but an improper, conniving American! But you must know, you show to the most excellent advantage, and any woman of sense would be about in her head to purchase any other!"

"And *you*, my dear—" He reached out and touched a gloved finger to her cheek.

Cat froze. Her whole being was one with that touch. She felt it flow through and fill her like Virginia sunshine, wrapping around her and warming her from head to heart to soul. She lifted her chin slightly and felt her eyelids falling closed.

"But later," his voice came softly. "Later."

His touch was gone. She opened her eyes, and he took her arm and immediately began walking again.

She felt as though her blood had been let, so great was her feeling of loss. Every step seemed to require more effort. In a flash she remembered the time long ago when a favorite doll had fallen into the fire, and realized that a grown woman mourns much the same way. Only the loss was different.

"There is yourself to consider," he said. "I am aware of your own desires, my dear, and I must remind you that I shall not travel the world, nor comply without a whimper should we disagree. I shall not be controlled by your purse, and shall be content to go on with my studies and my bees and my various other inglorious and sordid enterprises. I am not at all what you bargained for."

"No, you are not." She smiled up at him. "You are rather more. I have already crossed an ocean, you see, and you have shown me a gypsy. She read my palm. Would you like to know what she said?"

"Please."

"She said that the right man would cross water for me. I foolishly did not understand this at first. But *you* did cross water. You crossed the Wye to bring me back!"

His lips curled upward at the corners. "Ah, yes, when I said I must have my fortune told as well. I am completely convinced."

"You are too much the skeptic."

"Absolutely. And then we have still your father to think of, who I am persuaded must be pleased with your choice. And I, my clever Miss D'Eauville, would not meet with his approval. I am not speaking now of my lack of a highly regarded sire and dam, but of my personal merits. You must agree that today's debacle has put me at a disadvantage."

"Oh, but that is easily remedied. He must come to know you. I shall have a departure party before my journey to London—I am to have a shopping trip, you see—and you will all attend, you and your aunt and the Millingtons. Yes, everyone shall come. And you will be your charming and scholarly best with him."

"If I were so to elevate myself in his personal opinion, it would mean nothing if he has not modified his thinking on his requirements for your husband."

"Do not go in circles. It leads you nowhere. In any case, I have a further plan. You shall show your true mettle and rescue me from some horrid calamity. I have done some thinking on this, and have concluded that you must rescue me from kidnappers."

"Miss D'Eauville, here you are going too far. I have my limits."

"Oh, they won't be real kidnappers, of course. You will arrange it."

"What? I, arrange it?" He stopped and turned to her again. "I cannot possibly do such a thing!"

"Of course, you can. I leave the planning up to you. After all, you are a superior beast."

"No, I cannot do it, Miss D'Eauville. No—absolutely not!"

Cat gazed up into his eyes, noting the odd combination of perplexity and astonishment.

"I have faith in you," she said sweetly. "And now, I think we should go relieve your aunt and my father."

Chapter Seventeen

*T*he distraction of Lola's removal from the room did not last long enough for Bea. Finally there were only the two of them remaining—herself, and Lionel D'Eauville.

Bea gazed over the serving table and reached for the teapot. "Will you have more tea?"

"No, thank you. I have only begun to drink it."

Foiled there, she reluctantly withdrew her hand.

"Another biscuit?"

"I am afraid not. I do not eat much between meals. I like to stay fit."

"I daresay the children will be back soon."

A brief silence. Lionel shifted in the wing chair he was seated in, which seemed too small for his large frame.

"Miss Southrop," he said finally, "I am sorry for surprising you today. Truth be told, I did not know you were . . . still residing here."

"Oh, I see." Bea sipped her tea and stared at the gilt-framed landscape on the opposite wall. "I find I am not surprised."

"Please explain. Why are you not surprised?"

"Why would you think of such a possibility? You would not be so distracted from your plans of greatness!"

Bea's hand shook and her tea lapped at the rim of

her cup. She rested the cup once more, and then realizing she had no occupation for her hands, picked it up again.

"I do believe you are angry with me."

She inhaled. "Angry? On account of something that is years past? Nonsense. Like you, I do not think about it."

"Then look at me."

"Don't be foolish." *Dear God, what have I done? I cannot think. I shall have a heart seizure right here and now. I am a foolish, foolish old woman.*

"I am not being foolish. I would very much like to see your face. Look at me."

She did . . . slowly, after replacing her cup. She met the gaze of the only man who could make her heart turn over at a glance, the only man she had ever dreamed of at night, the only man to have shattered her heart into a thousand useless pieces.

His face was no longer smooth and youthful, but more angular and lined, the face of a man who had seen much of life. His hair, although still full and thick, had gone from a deep brown to brown thoroughly threaded with silver. But his eyes were still that rosewood brown, just the color of his daughter's eyes. And she still felt the excitement, the giddy promise of adventure she had felt when she had first gazed upon his face. Lionel was a man who had not lost his hunger for living life to the fullest.

"Why are you angry with me, Bea?" he asked.

She thought she would dissolve right there and flow off her chair into a puddle upon her poor dead sister's Aubusson carpet. But she was not so fortunate.

"Have you no feeling whatsoever?" she said. "I had three letters from you, then none at all. I learned from my sister, who had learned it from the late Lady Ralston, that you had wed in Boston. It was . . . was very ungraceful of you."

He took in a deep breath and sighed. Then he turned his great head and gazed out the French windows into the garden. "You were very young, Bea. I know . . . that there was the beginning of something between us, but I had nothing to give you. No title, no money, only my youthful energy. Here it would have gained me nothing." He paused, but spoke again in a moment. "My brother Frederick joined the navy, and where did that get him? He did not come home covered in laurels and bearing a fortune in prize money. He came home under the lily, and lay at rest in the family crypt at the age of two-and-twenty."

Bea swallowed. She was trembling, and hoped he would not notice it.

"Because your older brother died in service to the Crown did not mean you would also. In any case, you told me your father had planned for you to join the clergy."

Lionel harrumphed in derision. "Me? In the clergy? Not likely. Not only do I lack the temperament, I had no desire to live on a pittance. I certainly could not have wed on my salary—much less raise a family. And you knew my father. He was as tough and stubborn as they came. He would not have advanced me one penny."

"He was like you."

"What did you say?" Lionel turned to look at her.

She drew a slow breath, bravely holding his gaze. "He was—like you, Lionel. You may dislike it, but there is nothing to argue with."

He continued to stare at her for a moment, then slowly lowered his cup. "By all that is holy—"

"Do not speak so. Please."

"I think . . . you may be right."

Surprise made her hesitate. She breathed in. "Yes, I am right. You were every bit as determined, perhaps more, than he was. You decided to make your fortune in America, and that was the end of it. The desires of no one else had the least influence upon you."

Lionel cleared his throat. "I am sorry, Bea. Very sorry. I had no idea I did you such an injury."

She did not answer. She could not. She looked at her hands.

"As I explained, I saw no road for me here. When I arrived in Boston, my full focus was upon survival. My country of birth did me no favors. All the talk was of the French Revolution, and I made a decision never to reveal my heritage. I survived for some time as a dockhand before I had the good fortune of meeting Mr. Clemency Prescott, the owner of a large shipyard. And he had the kindness, and the foresight, to take me into his trade." Lionel paused. "I wed his daughter."

Silence fell. The hollow tick of the mantel clock filled the room. Bea clutched her handkerchief in her lap and begged her scattered wits to arrive at something to say. *Where* were the children?

"I see your nephew is well grown," Lionel said. "A very fine-looking young man, in spite of the curious costume he was wearing."

Thank God. Or perhaps she should thank Lionel for the rescue.

"He is an absolutely wonderful man. If I could choose among princes for a nephew, I would have no other. He is the kindest, most thoughtful nephew a woman could have, and he has my aunt's brilliant mind. If only he did not have such an aversion to . . ."

"To what?"

"I was going to say settling down. But I think he has lost his objection to it."

"Is that so? And who is the fortunate lady?"

Bea tipped her chin up. Now was the time for strength. If she owed nothing to his daughter, she did to her sister's son. "If she is allowed to have him, your daughter."

Silence. Bea hazarded a glance at Lionel's face. He looked much struck—and thoughtful.

"So the wind blows that way, does it? I feared as much."

Bea felt her anger and frustration growing, suddenly

and rampantly, growing until she could hold it no more. She looked him frankly in the eye.

"You feared it? *Feared* it? And what is so *undesirable* about my nephew that he deserves to be *feared* as a potential husband? He is worth one hundred of your— of your worthless Lord Johnstons! My nephew has not gone about begging, he has made his own fortune! He is a man worth—worth—"

"Hold, hold, Bea! God Almighty, I did not mean—"

"Yes, you did! You did. He is nothing because he does not own your precious title. A title that you yourself never had! You will destroy your own daughter's happiness for that one thing, and it is all from pride!"

"Bea . . . no, Bea. It is not from pride. It is for her. She deserves it, and I cannot give it to her. All my life . . ."

"All your life—" Her voice broke. She snatched her handkerchief to her eyes. "All your life . . ." she said brokenly, "you have thought of nothing but aggrandizing yourself. When you say you do it for others, that is nothing but an excuse. I once thought you a wise man, Lionel, but now I see how wrong I have been!"

The silence was ominous in the morning room when Cat and Lord Weyland returned from their walk. No one questioned why Lord Weyland still wore the same clothes. No one seemed to notice that Cat's cheeks were flushed pink. Even her father looked unusually grave.

Cat hazarded a glance at Lord Weyland, and he gently shook his head.

"I see you have finally returned," said her father. "We shall have our horses now, I think. Our visit has been overlong."

Cat and her father left, and she was even more concerned at his silence on their ride home. She could not learn a thing of the private moments her father and Miss Southrop had shared, and was left solely to speculation.

Still worse, her father's mood lasted for the next several days. He did enact a jolly demeanor for the other guests, but Cat knew he was not himself. In private, he volunteered nothing else. When he did speak, it was of the proposed shopping trip to London.

The very topic made Cat's heart sink.

It was then she put forth her idea of a farewell party before her journey, and was cheered when her father seized upon the idea. She met with some resistance when she insisted on sending invitations to everyone, including all in the Weyland household, but her father finally capitulated. Cat flew into full planning mode, engaging the enthusiasm of the unsuspecting Lady Ralston—and drawing the wary Becky—into her grand party scheme.

"For it is your farewell party, too," Cat told Becky one evening in Cat's chamber. "You need to shop for your trousseau also. We shall have such a time!"

Becky regarded her calmly and blinked from her seat by the fire. "I do not require so much," Becky said. "Certainly not grand gowns and hats. I will purchase fabric for some day dresses and the necessities, and some good warm wool for a cape, for it is so cold here. But Lord Rhodes and I plan on spending a good deal of time at home. It is what we like. And I want to become well acquainted with his dear children as soon as I may."

"That is all very well, so long as you come." Cat bent over her project, seated in a wing chair opposite Becky. Cat was working on refurbishing the trim on her favorite traveling hat, as the bronze-and-black plumes had become sadly bent and limp.

"Cat, my love, I do not understand why you are suddenly so happy about your match with Lord Johnston."

"Can I not decide to be happy? It is marriage I want after all, not a particular husband. I shall soon be exploring the most glorious reaches of—um—Italy. Yes, I shall go to Italy, and take a house by the ocean."

"You are funning with me."

"I am not."

"Cat, I have known you since you were three days old, and you are funning with me."

Cat looked up. "Very well. I may choose a different country. What does it matter? I shall be free."

"No, you will not. Not while you cannot have what you love."

Cat looked quickly down at her hat, and fiddled with the peacock feathers she had retrieved from Charles's lawn.

"I have known for many years now," Cat said quietly, "that I could not have what I loved. I was born female. Father loves me, but he will not give me the running of the shipyard."

"No, it is true, he will not. My brother Thomas shall have the running of it. But Thomas would welcome you there for visits and advice. You know him well enough to know that of him."

Cat sniffed. "He will be kind to me, then go about doing what he will. It is not the same thing at all. No, to be my own woman, I must go elsewhere, so I shall see the world. Father will be content, so why should I not be?"

"Why, indeed."

Cat did not respond, so Becky broke the silence.

"You are forgetting one thing. You are in love, and you are denying yourself that love. I have known this for many days—before, perhaps, you did yourself."

Cat sat still, staring at the hat.

"So tell me, dear, why are you so happy?" Becky asked.

Cat looked up, hoping her eyes did not appear over-bright. Even to her dear Becky, she never revealed her tears. "Very well, I shall tell you. It is because I hope that before many days, I shall be engaged to wed Lord Weyland. I simply wish that I had more than hope."

"Cat, love, it is time you trusted me again." Becky leaned forward and placed a hand on Cat's knee. "Tell me all, and let me see if I can help."

Cat was uneasy. Of late, she experienced more and more emotions that were not usual for her, and tonight, at her going-away ball, she was uneasy. Uneasy!

She had made her grand entrance downstairs that evening to the great admiration of all present, wearing an overdress of white net over apricot silk, and her mother's diamond necklet. Lord Johnston had greeted her with what seemed to be great affection, perfectly hiding any apprehension. From all sides she was greeted and toasted, and her father again enacted his role of jubilant father. For that matter, even Lord Macclesby had been courteous. He, with several of her other former husband candidates, had stayed, probably to take advantage of the feasting and entertainment while it lasted. Yet she could not believe Macclesby, in particular, to be anything but disappointed that she had not chosen him.

Everyone was acting a role, including herself. No one was what they seemed. Except, perhaps, Miss Millington . . .

She gazed across the ballroom to the place she had last seen Miss Millington, who had been standing with her mother, pink-cheeked and apparently happy, but the Millingtons were now lost in a sea of guests. Was Miss Millington perhaps the only one who presented herself as she was? Could she be looking forward to the evening to come with excitement, not trepidation? Cat surely hoped so. Becky had confided that Miss Millington confessed to nervousness, but felt she would do.

Then there was Miss Southrop . . . yes, she had come. Cat had breathed a sigh of relief to see her. Miss Southrop and her father were, as yet, dancing about each other so to speak, as if uncertain how to approach the other. But Cat noticed glances from one to the other,

when one supposed the other was not looking, and now
her father was standing closer to Miss Southrop than
he had earlier. Perhaps . . . yes, perhaps. Oh, she prayed
that it would come about!

Lastly, however, there was Lord Weyland. He was
his charming self, but quieter than usual. He had spoken with her briefly and of nothing at all, and drifted
on. That had distressed her the most. She did, at the
very least, wish to see him engage in conversation with
her father, but she had not noticed it if he had. As to
her idea that he might kidnap her, he had been most
uncooperative. It was most annoying that the fates of
all had been left to her own, and her dear Becky's, skill-
ful planning!

She could not tell if her strategy would succeed. That
was what unsettled her so. Patience had never been her
strong suit.

It was now, she believed, a quarter of an hour past
midnight. She had already danced several dances, and
had excused herself. Johnston had some time ago left
her with a glass of lemonade, which was getting un-
pleasantly warm; and now, fearing approach by another
guest, she decided to step out for some air.

She only made it a few steps down the hall when she
was approached by one of cousin Charles's footmen.

"Miss D'Eauville, I have a note." The liveried man
bowed and extended the tray. Cat took up the note and
unfolded it. She read,

> "My dear Miss D,
> I must speak to you in private about something of
> utmost importance. Please meet me in the garden
> near the bust of Caesar as soon as you read this.
> Yours, Johnston."

Her heart dropped. *Botheration.* What was the foolish
man thinking? And why had he written such a note,
and signed his full name? She could think of no good

reason why he should wish to speak to her privately at such a time, when it might have been arranged all day with less drama attending it. But if he wished to speak with her, she must by all means find him. She could not chance her plans going awry at this point.

"There is no answer. Thank you."

The footman bowed and went on his way. Cat paused, then continued down the hall and took the stair down one flight, then rapidly sought her room. She was visiting no bust of Caesar in the garden at midnight without being properly prepared.

Quickly, Cat donned a warm shawl and found her reticule. A moment later she reentered the hall, descended the last flight of stairs, and slipped out the door into the garden.

It was a coolish night. Cat drew up the shawl she had draped over her arms and padded softly down the stone steps from the terrace. At the bottom of the steps, she hesitated for a moment, then remembered where she had seen the bust of Caesar. It was along the walk not far from the terrace, where the path returned by the yew hedge. It was fortunate that this was not far, for there was little light to see save the backdrop of illumination from the windows of Ralston Hall.

As the path took its first turning, the pale light became blackness. Cat sighed in frustration and a little apprehension. She stopped. This was absurd. But recalling what was at stake, she pressed on. In a moment she saw the soft white glimmer of Caesar's face in the darkness.

She stopped when she reached the bust, then looked about herself. There was nothing to see but the blackness of the yew hedge.

"Lord Johnston?" She waited. Presently she thought she heard the sound of movement.

"Lord Johnston, is that you?"

There was no answer.

Chapter Eighteen

"*G*od Almighty, are you telling me that my daughter is missing?"

Lord Ralston swallowed and resisted an urge to loosen his neckcloth. Holding the incredulous stare of his American uncle, he cursed the day he had agreed to assist Miss D'Eauville's search for a husband.

"I do not know, for a fact. But a young lad who works in my stable insists he saw her taken off in a carriage. I was summoned to see him not a quarter hour past."

"Have you looked for her here?"

"No, not yet."

"Well, then, let us be looking for her! Let us not just stand here and prattle about it!"

"Yes . . . sir, but the boy is generally reliable."

"Are you saying you believe she has been *kidnapped*?"

Charles sent a furtive glance about them. They were standing outside the doorway to the ballroom, and although there was no one nearby, he saw glances being attracted by D'Eauville's loud voice.

"Sir, a little caution . . . is in order."

Lionel D'Eauville raked Charles with a thunderous expression, but when he spoke, it was with a lower, but equally lethal, voice.

"Where is Weyland?"

"Weyland, sir? I believe he was at billiards last. Shall I . . ."

But D'Eauville was already striding for the billiards room. Charles hurried after him.

"Why do you want Weyland? I am sure he can be of assistance, but—"

"I can tell you this much," said D'Eauville, sounding as if he were speaking through gritted teeth. "If my daughter is missing, *he* is responsible!"

Charles was helpless to do anything but follow his uncle into the billiards room. There was Weyland, in happy ignorance, taking his turn with a cue.

"Weyland!" D'Eauville bellowed.

Weyland spared him a glance. He looked somewhat surprised, but went back to lining up his shot. "One moment."

"I do not give you one moment! I will speak to you—"

Weyland took his shot. It banked nicely, and sank its target.

"—Now!" finished D'Eauville.

Weyland stepped back from the table and leaned his cue against the wall. All playing had stopped in the room, and those several gentlemen stood transfixed.

"What may I do for you?" Weyland asked.

"You can tell me the location of my daughter!"

Weyland blinked. He glanced at Charles. "In the ballroom, I presume."

Charles broke in. "Gentlemen, *please*," he whispered urgently. He beckoned to Weyland, who was already approaching. Charles stepped hurriedly forward to intercept him, and bent close to his ear. "My Timothy just informed me that he saw Miss D'Eauville taken away in a carriage."

Weyland felt his world come to a slow, careening stop. For a moment he thought that he had not heard the words Charles had spoken, but only imagined them.

"When?" Jack asked.

"Timothy told me only moments ago. It would have happened only shortly before that."

Good Lord, Jack thought. *She has done it. She has gone and had herself kidnapped!*

"Never mind all that," D'Eauville growled. "Tell me where you have taken her!"

D'Eauville had arrived at Charles's side. Jack looked back at the very angry face of Lionel D'Eauville, and realized the very delicate position he was suddenly in. It was complicated by his very real worry about Miss D'Eauville, even if she had got up this escapade by herself.

"Sir, I have taken her nowhere, nor do I have any knowledge of this."

"Weyland wouldn't do that sort of thing," Charles said quickly. He put himself forward, between D'Eauville and Jack. "I have known him all my life. And if he has taken her somewhere, then why is he standing here?"

D'Eauville frowned. He seemed, at last, to be reconsidering.

"We must look for her," Jack said. "First, let us find Johnston."

D'Eauville sighed. He stared at the floor a moment. The room was as silent as a tomb, so intent was everyone on D'Eauville's reply. Jack, for his part, remained braced to take the bruising punch the older man would most certainly deliver. Yes, Miss D'Eauville had upturned the punch bowl this time!

"Very well," D'Eauville said quietly. "I—I apologize, Weyland, if I have been out of line. I thought . . . well, it does not matter."

Jack breathed out in relief. "I understand."

"Jack," said Charles, "there is one other thing. Timothy said that Thomas told him that he saw the carriage pass Weyland Hall."

"Damn! It is going north!"

"What in blazes are you talking about?" roared

D'Eauville, his spirits instantly revived. "Who is Thomas? And how could he tell Timothy he saw the carriage from two miles away?"

Jack looked at D'Eauville. "Thomas is Timothy's twin brother. He works for me. There is an odd connection between them."

"Well, make sense! How could he—"

"Weyland is right," said Charles. "They seem to know what the other is thinking."

"I think you both are mad."

A sound came from the doorway behind them.

"Oh, thank God! There you all are!" Lady Ralston rushed into the room, followed by his aunt Bea. Jack saw his aunt hesitate when she spotted Lionel D'Eauville, then she picked up her chin and came determinedly onward.

Lady Ralston rushed to her husband's side and clung to his arm for support.

"She is gone, Ralston," she said. "Miss Millington is gone. We cannot find her anywhere. And where is Lord Johnston?"

When she had wished for adventure, kidnapping had not been what she'd had in mind. At least, not this *type* of kidnapping. There was no velvet-lined coach and richly garbed prince offering her sweets, and she must be riding in the most ill-sprung vehicle in the country.

She had been seized in the dark, rapidly conveyed to a closed carriage, and from there she had traveled more than a half hour; and given they were moving at all speed, Cat was feeling uncomfortably sore and battered.

When she saw Weyland again, she did not know if she would kiss him or give him a cuff on the ear! The wonderful man had done what she had asked after all—but he might have told his kidnapper-hirelings that they need not take such precautions with her!

Cat shifted her position on the floor of the bouncing carriage. She lay between the two seats, wrapped in the blanket, but the blanket was not tightly secured. She had been working on freeing herself since the carriage door had closed, and she thought the binding was about to come free.

Success! Cat felt the blanket loosen. With a little more effort, she writhed free and hoisted herself onto the seat. She raised the window shade and looked out, but there was nothing to see, save the blackness of a country night.

Well, now, Cat, what shall you do next?

There was nothing to do, of course, but wait for Weyland to arrive and effect a dramatic rescue. Cat sighed. It was all to good purpose, but in the ordinary way, she preferred to take some action herself.

The carriage was cold, so she felt the floor for the blanket. To her satisfaction, she found her reticule. Apparently, her kidnappers were not thieves. She cloaked herself in the musty old blanket again, and inspected the contents of her reticule. Finding it in order, she leaned back with a sigh and hoped Weyland would hurry.

When the carriage slowed, she sat up anxiously and peered out the window again. They appeared to be drawing up to a small farmhouse . . . no, a local inn. The door began to open, and she dropped the shade.

She did not see Weyland standing outside, but two of the masked men. She sat coolly, staring at them. They stared back, as if in some confusion.

"Do not stand there and stare all night," Cat admonished. "I freed myself, thank you, and I am highly annoyed. It was not at all necessary to truss me like a loin of pork."

One of the men found his voice. "No screechin' or carryin' on," he said. "We are changing carriages. I warn you, we are desperate men."

"Oh, do be quiet," Cat snapped. "I cannot think why we must change carriages. I certainly hope it is no worse than this one. Help me down."

They accommodated her, and treated her with complete courtesy this time. They led her across the yard to another carriage, which waited in the shadow of the inn.

"I should like another covering," Cat said. "This blanket smells of mice."

"Ain't got one. Sorry, miss."

They handed her up into the carriage and closed the door. In the darkness Cat smelled another scent—an odd, spicy odor, like the smell of an exotic tobacco. Then she noticed that she was not alone.

"Good evening, my charming Miss D'Eauville. I hope you are well."

Good Lord—Macclesby! Cat stared at the barely discernible image of the man in the dark, for a moment too stunned to speak. Then she grasped the meaning of it all.

"Lord Macclesby! I am so surprised! I never would have thought—"

"That it would be me?" He asked. "I did not believe that you would. Perhaps it is for the best."

"No, I would not have thought it at all. Oh, me!" She burst out laughing.

It was a moment before she contained herself and became aware of Macclesby's silence.

"I am sorry," she said. She hiccuped, and laughed again. "It is just that—of all persons who could be prevailed upon—to rescue me from Lord Johnston! It is just too amusing."

"I do not see why it is so amusing," said Macclesby, sounding miffed. "And I hardly was prevailed upon."

"Oh, dear, now I have wounded your feelings, and you are doing me a service. I thank you, most sincerely. I am most grateful."

He cleared his throat. "Then you are in favor of this?" He sounded somewhat surprised. "I had feared you might not be."

"Of course. I knew all about it, you see."

"You did?"

"Well, not all. I was not sure if it would happen. And I did not know that it would be you."

"Do you say it would not have mattered who it was?"

"Not particularly." Cat laughed again. "As long as I were kidnapped, it did not matter to me if it were by the devil himself! But I *do* object to this blanket!"

At Ralston, the gathering in the billiards room had grown larger, and had removed to the library where the family could have some semblance of privacy. Lionel D'Eauville, Lord Ralston, Lady Ralston, Lord Weyland, Miss Southrop, and Mr. and Mrs. Millington made up the group.

"It makes no kind of sense at all!" said D'Eauville. "Why would my daughter elope with her own fiancé?"

"What of *my* daughter!" huffed Mr. Millington. "She cannot have gone off by herself! We have looked everywhere!"

"No, she did not, because Miss Millington has gone with Johnston," Weyland said. "I am very sorry, Mr. Millington, but I have learned that your daughter and he have a preference for one another."

"But Johnston—and Miss D'Eauville—" Charles rubbed his forehead wearily, turned from the group and walked slowly away. "I am done for," he murmured as he passed Weyland.

"My daughter would not do such a thing as elope!" cried Mr. Millington.

"Well, then," barked D'Eauville, "who has *my* daughter?"

"But if I might speak," Mrs. Millington said. She turned to her husband. "My dear, Lord Weyland is quite right. Johnston and Augusta *did* have an acquaintance." Here she turned to Miss Southrop. "I am *so* sorry we shall not become related! And I must say"— she glanced at the group, now—"I am particularly sorry for Miss D'Eauville. Johnston *is* so exceptionally eligible! We must, of course, fetch the children back and do what must be done."

Miss Southrop cleared her throat. "My nephew," she said coolly, "is *more* than exceptionally eligible."

"I shall ride as soon as my horse is readied," Weyland said. He sent his aunt a look, hoping to staunch her motherly defense.

"I shall, also," snapped Mr. D'Eauville.

"That will not be necessary, sir. I will go faster alone."

"It is *my* daughter, and I shall go!"

Jack felt a tug on his sleeve, and he looked down into his aunt's concerned eyes. "Let him come," she said softly.

Jack hesitated. He was certain, nearly certain, that Miss D'Eauville was in no danger, but he could hardly convey that opinion to D'Eauville. And his aunt's expression spoke volumes. She was still in love with D'Eauville . . . and she had forgiven him.

"Surely you are riding after *my* daughter as well," said Millington.

Jack ignored him. "Mr. D'Eauville, will you follow in your carriage?"

"I shall come also," said Millington.

"What shall *I* do?" wailed his wife. "Oh, they will not be caught anyway! Only think, my little Augusta, a countess!"

"Ralston," Jack snapped at his friend. Charles, still gloomily staring at the blackness of the window, turned his head at the sound of Jack's voice.

"Ruined," he murmured.

Jack sighed in frustration. "Accompany Mr. Millington, if you would. And we will need another carriage, in case we part ways." Jack turned and strode out the doorway. Mr. D'Eauville followed.

"I prefer to ride, but you are right," D'Eauville said.

"We will need a carriage, and riding hard for long distances is for young men."

Jack stopped in the hall and turned to face D'Eauville. They regarded each other.

"Sir, I think you fully capable of riding hard for miles if you wished to do so," Weyland said.

"Age also brings wisdom. And if a younger man is willing to do something in my stead, I see no need to protest."

Weyland gazed at D'Eauville a moment longer, noticing for the first time the intelligent brown eyes that were so like his daughter's. Then Jack nodded. "Very well. I am on my way."

The expression in D'Eauville's eyes was to haunt Weyland. D'Eauville believed his daughter to be in true danger, and thought Weyland to be doing something heroic! It was nothing of the sort, for Miss D'Eauville had arranged her "abduction" by herself.

He was outside quickly enough, and found Timothy holding his mount.

"Is there anything more you did not tell Lord Ralston?" Weyland asked as he mounted.

"No, sir."

"You did not notice anyone else leave?"

"Yes, sir."

"Did you? And who was that?"

"I don't know 'is name, sir. Him with the long skinny shanks."

Macclesby.

"Thank you, Timothy," Weyland said grimly. He turned his horse and set off at all speed.

Weyland had the advantage of speed over D'Eauville and Millington, plus he had left ahead of them. Had he continued to believe that Miss D'Eauville had staged the kidnapping, he would not have been concerned about leaving the carriages, and his assistance, some way be-

hind him. However, now he feared a new possibility—
that Miss D'Eauville was in true jeopardy. Would Macclesby be capable of such a desperate act? The more
Weyland thought about it, the more convinced he became that Macclesby was. And that left him with no
choice but to ride as fast as he could and hope the
others would keep to his trail. It might not be an easy
one to follow.

Macclesby, if indeed it was Macclesby, had traveled
north. However, Miss D'Eauville was of age to marry,
if one disregarded her father's control of her inheritance—and one might if one were desperate enough,
hoping her father would loosen the purse strings once
the deed were done. In any case, Macclesby would not
need to take Cat to Scotland. That he had set their
course northward was a ruse to throw off any followers;
Weyland felt he would discover a clue or two along the
way left to make it appear that they traveled north,
but somewhere they would turn south and head for
Macclesby's estate. However, Weyland needed to be
certain.

For the next two hours Jack pushed Ptolemy hard,
slowing to rest the horse when he had to, and stopping
at every inn and alehouse he encountered on the route
north, asking after the two couples at every one. He at
last reached the small inn known as The Red Boar. He
had hopes of news here—the timing was right for a
change of horses driven from Ralston, and Jack knew
that the road forked ahead. One fork doubled back . . .
and with a little roundabout journeying, could ultimately take Macclesby home.

Jack strode inside the inn, bending his head to keep
from bumping his skull on the low-beamed ceiling.
Through the wood smoke he spotted the proprietor,
serving a rather rough-looking band of three locals at
one table.

The proprietor approached him. "Good evenin', sir."

"Good evening. I am looking for a party who might have passed this way. Two parties, in fact."

The proprietor looked concerned. "I dunno. Been a few folks here tonight."

"One gentleman is tall, well-dressed, and could be described as handsome, accompanied by a blond young lady in a white formal gown."

The proprietor shrugged. "Not as I recall."

"The other couple was a tall thin man and a tall young woman, dark hair, well dressed."

"No, sir—I think not."

Jack hesitated. "Come, man! You must have seen someone!" Jack produced a coin from his purse and held it up. "A thin man, with enough ruffles to give his valet a headache. Think!"

The proprietor's eyes widened. "Oh, yes! They were here. Headin' north, he says. In a hurry, he says. I didn't see the lady. He got somethin' for the missus to take in the carriage."

"I see. You are certain they went north?"

"Yes, sir, I am."

Jack left the inn, feeling a little discouraged. It did sound as if the proprietor was talking about the correct couple, but he had almost seemed a little too ready with the information once the reward had been offered. But north? It was possible, but not necessary. Macclesby had only to see that Miss D'Eauville was sufficiently compromised, which could be done in the comfort of his home—and accomplish his end much sooner. Perhaps . . .

Jack waved at a young lad who peered at him from around the corner of the inn.

"Young lad! Come here. I need assistance."

The boy looked hesitant until Jack took a coin from his purse. The boy approached cautiously, then stood several paces away, looking at him.

"A carriage came this way tonight. I believe it

stopped here. A young lady was in it—very striking, tall with dark hair. There was also a tall, very thin gentleman . . . he may have been with her, or he may have been waiting here. I do not know. But I would like to know which way they went."

The boy looked cautiously back at the inn, then at Jack. "It 'ud be worth somethin.' "

"I have something." Jack showed the boy the coin.

The boy held out his hand.

"Speak first."

The boy swallowed. "Was 'e spindly legged?"

"Yes."

"Is she a miffy 'un?"

Jack almost smiled. "Absolutely. Well?"

"He was here waitin'. She got out of her carriage and into his. Then they went—" He pointed. "Down that road."

"Was she well?"

The boy tilted his head. "She was rare tiffed. She give a jaw t' the gentlemun what come with her. And I ain't sayin' nothing else."

"That will do." Jack flipped the boy a coin. "Many thanks."

He strode up to his horse, and patted him on his sleek neck. "And on we go, Ptolemy," he said. He mounted quickly, and rode the way the lad had pointed.

Chapter Nineteen

*H*e found them much sooner than he expected. The disabled carriage loomed suddenly in the dark, tilted at a crazy angle in the ditch at the side of the road. In the clouded light of the moon, he could scarcely see it at all.

A new fear constricted his throat. Without a thought of caution, he rode up to the carriage and slowly circled it.

"Hold, or I will shoot your barmy 'ead off!"

Jack wisely halted his horse. The voice had come from the darkness of the field. Looking carefully, he made out several shadowy shapes near the road.

It occurred to Jack that he could not be seen any more than they could see him, and if he successfully disguised his voice, he might make a better assessment of the situation.

Jack pulled his kerchief over his mouth, and attempted to lower his voice. He succeeded in introducing some huskiness into it. "I thought perhaps you might need assistance."

A hesitation. "No," came a gentleman's voice. *Macclesby*. "Thank you, but we do not. One of my men has gone to the wheelwright's, and we are comfortable enough."

"Perhaps," Jack said, "there is a lady who wishes to be conveyed to shelter."

"Oh, no thank you!" Miss D'Eauville's voice sang out. "We are expecting assistance. I should rather wait here."

She was here! Jack felt both relief and worry. Her voice had been strong enough, even cheerful, but he knew his Miss D'Eauville well enough to know she was more courageous than many men.

Jack thought rapidly. He was at something of a disadvantage, after all; although they could not identify him, the pale moon was at their backs. While they were but indistinct silhouettes to him, he must be somewhat visible to them.

"Very well," Jack said. There was nothing to do but ride on, and so he did. He proceeded some twenty yards down the road, then guided Ptolemy quietly down the bank and into the dark field. He would circle the kidnappers, thus take the same advantage that had worked against him.

He had the cover of trees for some distance. When he reached the verge, he was very near Miss D'Eauville, Macclesby, and whatever ne'er-do-wells he had hired.

Jack was not in the habit of carrying a pistol when attending a house party, so he was left armed only with his wits. With a little luck, this was weapon enough against Macclesby. But he sorely regretted leaving the carriages in his dust now; he could use Lionel D'Eauville's strength and stubborn courage at his back.

He dismounted, left Ptolemy standing quietly in the trees, and crept softly through the grass, approaching the men from behind. Ah, if all his hard-gained knowledge were now to be put to waste by a ball of lead! But his course was as set as if drawn by the hand of fate.

The only thing he *must* not do was to endanger Miss D'Eauville . . . but she would know how to keep out of the way. For God's sake, he hoped she would!

There were only three—Macclesby, one flunky, and Miss D'Eauville. He saw her now, where he had not before. She was seated in the grass, wrapped to her neck in something dark in color. He could see a pale patch where her dress peeped out, but she was otherwise as hidden as a doe in a thicket. Macclesby stood near her side, and the other man some paces closer to the road. Jack saw the flash of metal in his hand.

Jack drew a silent breath, then leveled his walking stick at the flunky.

"You, there! Drop your weapon!"

Macclesby and his henchman wheeled to face him. In a flash, Jack was pinned by three sets of astonished eyes.

"My musket is at the ready," Jack said, "and I am fully prepared to discharge it. I would suggest you do as I say." He paused. How odd it all seemed . . . and somehow, unreal. His own voice surprised him—cool and commanding, it was a voice that would have made his admiral grandfather proud.

"You by the road! Drop your weapon and step back. I give you to the count of three. One . . . two . . ."

The man dropped his pistol and took three steps backward.

"Damn you!" muttered Macclesby.

Jack was not certain if it were himself or the henchman who was being damned. He took it with equanimity. He was in control, and that, by God, was all that mattered.

"You two gentlemen shall now begin to back toward the road. The young lady will stay where she is."

It was going too well. The henchman, likely seeing no profit in risking his neck, continued to back up. And Macclesby, being a coward, did also.

Jack congratulated himself, and the thrill of a dangerous victory surged through his veins. He felt allpowerful. He felt the primitive, yet thrilling swell of maleness. He was a conquering Hun. He was a fearless Viking. He was a naked blue-painted Celt with the taste of blood in his mouth.

All this came to an abrupt end when the clouds

shifted. There he stood in moonlight, victoriously holding his quarry in the dead aim of his walking stick.

"You blithering fool!" cried Macclesby.

This time, Weyland *did* care whom Macclesby was calling a fool. For Macclesby had pulled a pistol from his coat.

Miss D'Eauville leapt to her feet.

"Miss D'Eauville, stay down!" Jack cried.

"Oh, both of you be done with it," snapped Miss D'Eauville. "I have been entertained quite long enough."

Jack and Macclesby looked at Miss D'Eauville at the same moment. Macclesby's pistol remained pointed at Jack.

"You said you wished to come," Macclesby said.

"Well, I have come quite far enough! I am cold, and I smell like a henhouse. Lord Weyland, please instruct Lord Macclesby that he may consider me rescued and be done with it."

Jack cleared his throat. "My dear, if you cannot instruct him yourself, I assure you that *I* cannot do it."

She looked at him, and he could imagine the puzzlement in her eyes. "Did not you arrange for him to abduct me?"

"Miss D'Eauville, I assure you I did not. His intent is quite real."

For a brief moment she continued to stare at Jack. Then, suddenly, she turned to Macclesby—and extended her arm straight. The moonlight flashed off metal in her hand.

"Lord Macclesby," she said sharply, "you will drop your pistol. *Now*."

Macclesby stared at her as if she were a three-headed goat. "You would not shoot me!"

"I shall not kill you," she said, "but I most assuredly will shoot you. The only question you should ask is— what part of you shall I shoot?" Delicately, she lowered her aim.

"Good God!" Macclesby cried. He dropped his pistol.

"Weyland, you may have this she-devil, and welcome!"
With that, he took to his heels and ran for the road.
His henchman fled before him.

They waited, and the sound of running steps faded
in the distance.

Jack sighed and turned to his love. She was quite
calmly secreting her tiny pistol in her reticule.

"I do not know," Jack said, "whether to kiss you, or
do something rather less pleasant to you."

"I suggest the kiss," she said.

He needed no further urging. She came into his arms,
henhouse smell and all, and the ragged blanket fell
away as he enveloped her in his embrace. He crushed
her close, found her lips, and kissed her in the light of
the fickle moon.

He released her mouth at last, and she gazed up at
him and gasped for breath. Then she laughed.

"If you could have seen yourself standing there with
that walking stick—"

"Believe me, I had a very accurate mental picture
of myself."

"Oh, but I am so *proud* of you! I have never seen
anything so courageous!"

If Jack had doubted the manliness of his rescue tech-
nique, all his misgivings were put to rest. His darling
had saved the day, of course, but her glowing praise
made him feel the very greatest of men. He decided he
was not the Hun or the Celt. He was Wellington.

Certainly such a man deserved another kiss!

Even Charles's well-sprung carriage was an unpleasant ride at the pace they were traveling. Bea clung
tightly and uttered no complaint. Her head was full
of swirling thoughts—that her nephew was somewhere
ahead on horseback, pursing Miss D'Eauville and her
kidnapper; that Lord Millington was somewhere behind
them, following his daughter's trail; that Lionel D'Eauville was beside her, grimly silent.

He had allowed her to come. He had seemed, almost, as if he had *wanted* her to come. The reason was a mystery whose answer eluded her, and the question tormented her with the rest.

"I say," Charles said from the seat facing them, "can it really be that Macclesby is behind this? He left early, it is true, but he may have become tired of it all."

"No one else is gone but Johnston," D'Eauville said. "You may draw your own conclusions."

Charles fell silent again.

D'Eauville stared out the black window. Then he sighed.

"It is my fault," he said quietly.

Bea looked at him. She saw the dark outline of his great form . . . and she seemed to feel a different emotion from him. Weariness. Defeat.

Bea licked her lips. "How can you say that?" she asked.

He paused before answering. Then he said, "I can because it is true. I sent her here to make a show of herself. You are quite right about me. My pride is my undoing."

A wave of surprise took her, and then, remorse.

"She wanted to come."

"She would do anything for me. Ambition is my fault, not hers."

"I almost had Johnston for her," Charles muttered. "I almost had him!"

"Lionel," Bea said softly, "she did not know what she wanted. You know that as well as I. She thought it as likely she would find it in England."

There was a short silence.

"You are kind, Bea," he said. "And in spite of how I have treated you. I had denied to myself . . ." He paused, and took a breath. ". . . that you could feel any attachment to me. I convinced myself that . . . the only feelings were mine."

Her heart swelled with a mix of sweetness and heartrending sadness. After all these years, Lionel was here, admitting what she had always wondered about, answering the question she had asked herself over and over these many years.

Perhaps it was because she was overcome with emotion and worry. Perhaps it was because she was nearly one and forty and well past shyness. But she lifted her gloved hand and rested it lightly on his arm.

"It is done now," she said. "And you have a grown daughter whom you love."

She felt a quiver run through him. "And now," he said huskily, "I may lose *her*!"

He pressed his great hand over hers. And the bond that was lost a lifetime ago came back, sure and warm and strong. "Bea," he said. "Please forgive me. I have made such great mistakes . . . but I am learning."

She filled completely—with pain, joy, loss, love, regret . . . thankfulness.

She gave his arm a reassuring squeeze. "If I know your daughter, and I believe I do now, as she is so much like you—she will be fine. I have every faith in her."

His breath caught. When he was able to speak, he said, "I shall not—ask for more. Well . . . and happy. Yes, that is what I want . . . for my little girl. That is all."

There was a shout from above, and the carriage abruptly began to slow.

"We are stopping!" cried Charles. He was upon his feet, prepared to exit the carriage as soon as he could. Bea, realizing what he had overheard, could not even blush. Her thoughts were with what lay in the road ahead.

It was not at all what they expected.

Lionel and Charles descended from the carriage, and stared up the road.

"Well, I'll be," said Lionel.

Bea stuck her head out the carriage door. "Let me

down! Oh, never mind, I shall help myself!" She began to attempt just that, and Lionel seized her around the waist and lifted her down, for all the world as though she were as light as thistledown. She found her footing beside him, breathless.

"Look," he said softly.

She peered ahead in the dark. The ghostly shapes of a man and a woman walked toward them, their arms linked intimately about each other, a horse following behind. It took her only a moment to know for certain. It was her Jack—and Miss D'Eauville.

Lionel started forward, drawing Bea with him. "Cat! Dear girl, are you well?"

She laughed as they met. "I am quite well, Father," rang out her gay voice, "and I have had such a fine adventure!"

Releasing Bea, Lionel enveloped his daughter into a hug.

"As long as you are well," Lionel said. His deep voice was husky with passion, and Bea blinked back a tear.

"As long as you are well," Lionel said again, his voice muffled against his daughter's hair. "My dear, I must speak with you. There are things you must know."

Jack stood by, holding Ptolemy, and glanced at Bea. She, being his aunt, understood his uncertainty. She gave him a reassuring smile, thankful he could not make out her tears. Then she went up and put her arms around him. "I am very proud of you," she whispered, and hugged him warmly.

Cat smiled, snug against the warm folds of her father's coat, his heart beating beneath her cheek. "You are going to tell me," she said into the cloth of his cravat, "that Johnston and Miss Millington have run off together."

Her father leaned back and stared down into her eyes. "You know that?"

"I am quite clever, Father. I am your daughter, you know."

"So you are," he said. "So you are!" and he laughed.

And Bea thought she had never heard such a lovely sound as Lionel and his daughter laughing together.

Much later the group sat together in the library before a comfortable fire. The house was now silent save for themselves, the guests having either departed or gone to their chambers. Mr. and Mrs. Millington had not yet returned; Cat surmised that they would not, and would later surface to present their daughter, the countess, and her new husband.

For herself, her heart was full with joy and hope. She allowed Jack to tell their story, and added her own version of events; and then, against Jack's protests, related her conviction of Jack's heroism. Her father laughed heartily at the tale.

"Now, I have something to tell you," he said. "My darling daughter, I have been taught a humbling lesson. I have decided that you must follow your heart, and if the young man of your choosing will kindly request your hand, I will assent." He looked at Lord Weyland. "Miss Southrop assures me you are quite extraordinary, Weyland, as has my daughter."

"Oh, Father!" Cat leapt up, and her father gained his feet in time to receive her in his arms. She kissed him soundly on both cheeks, and then flew back to Weyland, who was now standing as well, and seized his arm. She grinned up at Jack, and he smiled back at her. But there was something else in his eyes, now . . . an unease, a shadow of doubt. Drat, but the man was so very *English*! What could the matter be now? Would she *never* win him?

Then her father spoke again. "I have one more thing to say," he said. He stood, took two steps to the next chair, and then went down on his knee before Miss Southrop.

"If you will have me, Bea, I will make you the happiest wife in the world. That I promise, with all my heart."

Miss Southrop first looked astonished, then cried "Yes!" And as Cat's father gathered her into his arms, Miss Southrop wept in happiness.

Cat watched the reconciliation of her father and step-mother-to-be and felt a mist come to her eyes. If only . . .

But she did not need to make the next move. Jack took Cat's hand, and she followed him out of the room, her heart thudding heavily in her breast, feeling some inexplicable agitation when she knew . . . she *knew* Jack loved her . . .

Upon gaining the stairs, they found a morose Charles behind them.

"I am undone," he moaned.

Cat turned to him with some impatience. "Do not be absurd, Charles. Of course you are not. My father will not let Ralston fail."

Charles looked at her hopefully. "You think not?"

"Absolutely. He is quite amenable now, you see. And I know my father. He will quite like to be known as the D'Eauville who saved Ralston!"

"Do you say?" Charles looked much struck, and then he smiled. "If that could only be!"

"Go and speak to him," Cat urged. "Quickly. At this moment, he would give the moon and stars away!"

As Charles departed she turned to Jack, and would have seized his arm if he had not recaptured her hand first.

"Is that true?" asked Jack. "Will your father help Charles?"

Taking a calming breath, she gazed into his serious gray eyes and realized this was one reason she loved him. He was so conscientious, so loyal—so steadfast.

"Yes," she said.

"You are certain?"

"Absolutely. When my father's heart is turned, he is the most generous creature on earth."

He sighed. Then he led her down the stairs and out into the waning night.

Alone in the garden at last, Jack turned to her and placed his hands on her shoulders.

"My darling Miss D'Eauville," he said softly.

Her heart leapt. A shiver ran over her skin, as though her woolen shawl might not cover her shoulders, but it did.

"My darling Jack." She smiled up at the warmest gray eyes she knew, for the sky was paling, and she could see his dear face clearly. "You may call me Cat now." She tipped up her chin and closed her eyes, ready for another kiss.

"No, first I must ask you a very important question."

She opened her eyes again. "What is it?"

"Actually, I have several questions." His eyes twinkled down at her, and she knew she was in for a tease.

"What of adventure? I am a boring old fellow. I plan on staying here and puttering around with my animals and bees and experiments. And I am afraid I am not in favor of your traveling to the reaches of Africa alone."

She raised her brows. "Well, I think I have had quite enough of adventure for a while. I have crossed an ocean, met some very exotic and atrocious gentlemen, walked over a crumbling old bridge, had my fortune told by a gypsy . . ."

"There was the little matter of an abduction."

"Yes, there was that. I shall be content for a while. And then I shall demand something."

"Perhaps an elephant ride?"

"Oh, I do not know. I think I shall make you take me to a balloon ascension. I want to see England from the sky."

He smiled. "Done. But I am still fearfully wondering . . . what of your list?"

She stared at him. Then she laughed again. "Oh, dear! I had forgotten it! Is that not the most astounding thing?

Well, my dear Jack, it will soon be ashes in my grate. I shall make an entirely new one."

"Oh?"

"Yes. And guess whose name shall be the only one upon it?"

He kissed her, for he knew the answer.

And Cat settled against him, feeling his heart beat against hers, feeling the comfort of his arms holding her, feeling the wonder of his kiss, a pleasure still new.

She drew away slightly at last, and gazed seriously into his eyes. "Jack . . . what of your final question?"

"My final question . . . ?"

"The one you have not yet asked."

For a moment he looked confused—and then stricken.

"Good Lord," he said, half to himself. Then, "What can I have been thinking? You have me completely bewitched. I do not know my head from my—er—"

"The part of you that the queen shall heretofore never see?"

He chuckled softly. "Ah, my American enchantress! Yes, quite. Love of my life, soul of my soul, Psyche to my Cupid—"

She cut in. "Yes?"

His face went solemn. Then, softly, he asked the question she was waiting to hear. "Will you not marry me?"

"With the greatest pleasure! Now you really *must* go and ask my father!" But she presented her face for another kiss, delaying that important moment just a bit longer, and they embraced as the rosy dawn broke across the eastern sky.

He was such a sweet, foolish man, her Jack, she thought. But how was he to know that he was adventure enough for her, and more? For she would look forward to it daily, all the rest of their lives together.

Allison Lane

"A FORMIDABLE TALENT...
MS. LANE NEVER FAILS TO
DELIVER THE GOODS."
—*ROMANTIC TIMES*